MOJAVE GUNS

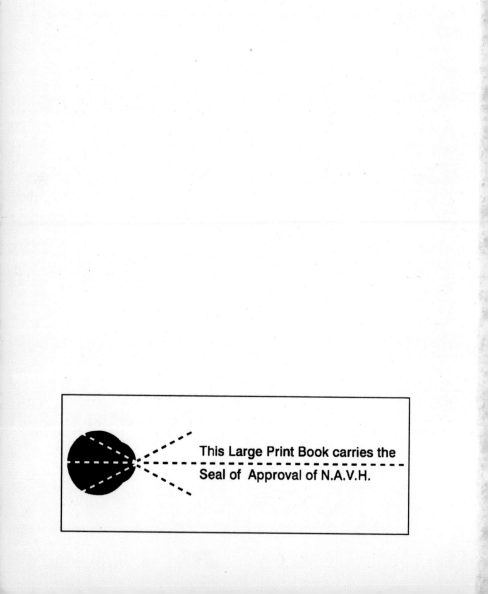

This Large Print Book carries the
Seal of Approval of N.A.V.H.

Mojave Guns

Roe Richmond

WHEELER PUBLISHING
A part of Gale, Cengage Learning

GALE
CENGAGE Learning·

Detroit • New York • San Francisco • New Haven, Conn • Waterville, Maine • London

LIBRARY OF CONGRESS CATALOGING-IN-PUBLICATION DATA

Richmond, Roe.
   Mojave guns / by Roe Richmond.
      pages ; cm. — (Wheeler Publishing large print western)
   ISBN 978-1-4104-5290-0 (softcover) — ISBN 1-4104-5290-5 (softcover)
   1. Large type books. I. Title.
PS3535.I424M65 2012
813'.54—dc23   2012030214

Published in 2012 by arrangement with Golden West Literary Agency.

Printed in the United States of America
   1 2 3 4 5   16 15 14 13 12
FD297

MOJAVE GUNS

CHAPTER I

Fifty miles west of the railhead, Montrill began to look for the detail that was to meet him halfway to Fort Burnside. It had been a slow grinding march with three heavy-laden wagons and insufficient escort, with hostile eyes on them every foot of the distance. He had two sergeants and eighteen troopers to convoy a cargo that might well change the complexion of the entire Indian campaign in Arizona. And they had to protect Major Thurston's daughter in the bargain.

They were picked men, to be sure, but there were not enough of them. There were never enough, Montrill thought with restrained bitterness. The Old Man couldn't spare any more, even to safeguard his own child and a shipment of arms and ammunition. Not that Teresa was exactly a child, Montrill reflected with a wry smile. He'd never understand why a girl like Teresa Thurston didn't stay back East where she belonged. Perhaps it was Herrold who brought her again to this frontier land. With Tess you always looked for the motivation in some man, and Crispin Herrold had been her chief interest at Burnside.

Riding at the point, Montrill twisted lithely in the hot sweated leather and glanced back along the mule-drawn, dust-drenched wagons, laboring in the furnace glare of the afternoon. Seaver and Dunleavy were out with the flankers, and Crater was bringing up the rear guard. Three of the best men in the Third, or any other outfit, but spread awfully thin here. Montrill wondered why the Apaches hadn't hit them. All across the scorched sand-and-rock wastes of the Mojave Desert, they had seen Indian smoke and felt Indian eyes on them, and through his glasses Montrill had caught occasional distant glimpses of brown-skinned warriors, but they hadn't yet closed in. Possibly they were waiting for the more broken terrain into which the column was now winding.

The slim blonde girl on the seat of the lead wagon waved almost gayly at the lieutenant. Montrill saluted briefly and went on scanning the bleak sun-blasted land-scape, spiked with cactus, cholla and yucca, rearing with stone columns and red buttes, slashed with dry arroyos and narrow rock-walled canyons. Whatever you thought of Tess Thurston's flirtatious, fickle ways, you had to admire her spirit and courage. In all this heat, discomfort, and danger, she was cheerful and vivacious, dainty and undaunted. There was something about army women that you seldom found elsewhere. Still Montrill resented her presence, wished she had remained in Emma Willard's Female Seminary at Troy, New York.

Dallas spoke, in his lazy Texas drawl, at Montrill's side: "They like to keep us sweatin', waitin' and wonderin', I reckon."

Montrill nodded. "That's it, Tex. If they hold off until that detail comes up, it will help." He never stood on rank or ceremony in the field, a fact that West Point associates like Herrold protested with outraged vehemence. But it had never lessened Montrill's authority, nor cost him any respect. The enlisted men liked Monty and would follow him, as old Seaver put it, into Hell's lowest pit and back.

"If they knew what was in them wagons, they wouldn't hang back." Tex Dallas grinned and spat tobacco juice.

Montrill smiled gravely, recalling that his verbal orders from Major Thurston had included a grim command: *"You will fight to the last man, if necessary, and fire the wagons as a final resort.*" Put the major's daughter on top of that, and you had a real nice assignment. Hardly surprising that Montrill's gray eyes were sunken, burning like live coals, his lean cheeks hollowed, the broad mouth thinned against his teeth.

In 1873, Winchester had patented a new repeating rifle, lever action, .44-40 caliber, far superior to any other such weapon in use. The army had taken a few on trial, and commanders throughout the West had clamored for these carbines at once. Ironically enough, the Indians often had better firearms than the United States Cavalry, Henry repeaters against the single-shot Ward-Burtons, Spencers and Remingtons that the military, loath as ever to change, persisted in issuing after the War of the Rebellion.

Only a limited number of the new Winchesters filtered through to western outposts where they were so direly needed, and most of them came through channels other than government issue. Thurston, for instance, had secured enough repeaters to arm small special details like the one Montrill was leading today, contrary to strict regulations but a lifesaving expedient. The Old Man, it was rumored, had paid for these from his own funds. . . . Now in the spring of 1875, two years after the rifle had been placed on the market and a full decade after Appomattox, some wilful and intrepid Washington officer had sheared away sufficient red tape so that Fort Burnside was receiving a consignment to arm two whole companies.

And how they'd gnash their teeth and tear their hair in the capital, thought Montrill, if they could see that precious shipment freighted through Apache country with an escort of but twenty-one! . . . Yet Thurston had been correct in his judgment. With the Indians getting bolder by the day, he had to keep patrols out constantly in the Cherokee Valley and in the Osage Mountains, at the same time manning the garrison. Of three original troops, he had only two left for active duty. The losses had been that heavy. Outnumbered as the army was, they might have been much worse.

Yes, the Old Man had done the best he could, giving Montrill quality if not quantity. Non-commissioned officers such as Dunleavy and Seaver were the backbone of any fighting force, and they were supported by enlisted men like Charley Crater and Tex Dallas, Emmett and Flint and Hendree, Slats Dillon, Red Fennell, Tut Jarnigan, Silk Slocum, and the rest. Tough and seasoned veterans, smart and resourceful, full of fire

11

and drive and the pride that never let a man slack off or quit. Fifty-cents-a-day men, that no amount of money could buy.

Rick Montrill himself was big and rangy, long and loose-limbed in the saddle, wide at the shoulders, flat and trim at waist and hips. The hair under the stained campaign hat was a tawny brown, sun-streaked to gold, and his eyes were gray flecked with green in the bronzed, angular, strong-boned face. He rode shirt-sleeved in the heat, the once blue shirt and trousers faded and dusted gray. There were no shoulder bars on the blue coat tied to the cantle. Although rated the best field officer at Burnside, Montrill was still a second lieutenant. In the War Between the States he had fought on the losing side, and out here he had worked his way up from the ranks. He wasn't likely to go any higher, fortunate to be commissioned at all. There were former Confederate officers of high rank riding as common troopers on the frontier.

Montrill had gone into the war as a boy of eighteen, serving in Stuart's cavalry and with John Mosby's guerrillas. He had been wounded at Spottsylvania two days after Jeb Stuart was killed. Later in the war, fighting with Forrest's cavalry under Hood, Montrill had suffered another wound in the terrible slaughter at Nashville. That ended the war for him, and four months later Lee had surrendered and it was all over. Montrill returned to his family home on the Chattahoochee, outside of Atlanta, but Sherman had been there and left nothing but blackened cellarholes and charred rubble.

His parents were dead and buried, he learned, his sisters married and gone, and Rick Montrill felt like a broken old man at twenty-two. He drifted westward with his younger brother Lance, and they finally joined the cavalry to fight Indians. Soldiering was the only trade either of them knew. . . . Now Rick was thirty-two, and Lance had been killed in action five years ago, under circumstances that Rick Montrill would never be able to forget or forgive.

CHAPTER II

"Rick, please!" Teresa Thurston's voice came through the clopping hoofs, rattle of wheels and creak of axles, rousing Montrill from his morbid reverie. He turned impatiently to look back through the dust haze and shimmering heat waves. The girl beckoned and Montrill reined up with a sigh, to wait until the wagon lumbered alongside. "Why don't you talk to me, Rick?" she asked, leaning toward him and smiling brightly, her deep blue eyes quizzical and a trifle taunting, her ripe lips full and lush in a petulant half-pout.

"Tonight, Tess."

"You didn't talk much last night."

"What is there to talk about?"

She laughed at him. "You aren't *that* old, Rick!"

"Old enough," Montrill said soberly. "I've got to stay on the lookout, Tess. We might have company any time."

"How has Cris Herrold been doing the past year?"

"All right. As good as any of us, I guess."

Teresa shook her fair head in mock dismay and tried again: "Is Kirby Tisdale still at the Flying F?"

Montrill nodded, remembering now that the major's daughter had also been interested in the foreman of Forrester's ranch that lay near the post. Tisdale had a cattleman's scorn for the military, and made no pretense of hiding it.

"You disappoint me, Lieutenant," the girl said. "I thought all Southern gentlemen were supposed to be charming conversationalists."

"Not any more," Montrill told her. "Or maybe it was a myth in the beginning."

Teresa gestured with annoyance. "There *is* something to be said for Academy men!"

"Definitely," he agreed, smiling. "Perhaps we'll have one with us before long."

"That will certainly make this trip more pleasurable. I suppose Jim Raven's daughter is still at Burnside? Dark and sultry and beautiful as ever." When Montrill nodded to this, the girl went on: "Well, that may account for your indifference."

"I'm not indifferent, Tess. I just have a lot on my mind. You'll excuse me, please?"

15

Montrill raised his hat and rode on ahead, with Teresa's dark blue eyes fixed somewhat spitefully on his high broad-shouldered back.

After a moment she shrugged, settled back and tried to relax on the hard jolting seat. Why should I worry about that broken-down old Rebel? thought Teresa Thurston. Cris Herrold is much younger, handsomer, more intelligent and refined, far more gallant and exciting. Look at Montrill with those enlisted men, just like one of them. He always preferred their company to that of his fellow-officers — and even to mine. Just as he favors that dark, strange, half-wild Anita Raven over me. . . . Well, if a man has low tastes, there isn't much you can do about it.

Montrill was wondering who would lead the detachment out to meet them. Ashley, he hoped. Ash was the best of the lot. Anybody but Crispin Herrold. Yes, even that bull of a Shaddock. . . . It couldn't be Barron, fortunately; he was still post adjutant, tied to the desk and the paper work for which he was best suited. The Old Man knew his subordinates all right, and where and how to use them. All except young Herrold. There was a problem that would baffle almost any C.O., and it was the army's fault that such a situation existed. There had been too many Herrolds at Burnside, and therein lay the whole trouble. Crispin's father and elder brother had preceded him at this same outpost, and the records they had left placed the last Herrold under an insupportable handicap.

Montrill could sympathize with Cris Herrold, feel sorry for the boy, but he could not like him nor work in harmony with him. The truth of the matter was Herrold wouldn't *let* anyone like him or get close to him. Whoever tried it was immediately chilled, cut to the quick, and frozen out. Cris Herrold was aloof and fiercely independent, Lucifer-proud and self-sufficient, the most completely isolated individual that Montrill had ever seen. Only with the opposite sex, with girls like Tess Thurston and Anita Raven, as different as they were, did Herrold lower the barrier and open up to some extent.

Stationed somewhere else, clear of the shadows left by his father and brother, Crispin Herrold might have been all right, an agreeable normal young man and an excellent officer, Montrill thought. The boy had talent and courage, a keen quick brain and a flair for leadership. Perhaps he went too much by the books, but in this type of warfare a man outgrew that — or he didn't last long. Herrold was smart enough to learn, develop and adapt himself to environment, anywhere else but at Burnside. With all the bases scattered around the continent, it seemed as if the army could have assigned him to some other camp.

Now Fennell rode in at a run from the right flank and pulled up at the head of the column, his hair fiery red under the rakehell slant of his hat, which disturbed certain officers from the Point. "Looks like they're closing in a little, sir. Seaver thinks they may be getting ready to strike before sundown." He had a well-bred Yankee accent.

Montrill considered this with somber briefness. "Tell Seav not to make a stand out there. If they start moving in, you're to fall back on the wagons, after a token resistance to slow them down. We'll make our fight here in a body. We should be able to hold them until relief comes."

Fennell nodded, saluted jauntily, and turned back into the tumbled boulders and low-lying reddish hills to the north. Montrill glanced at Dallas. "Tex, relay that order to Dunleavy. Tell him to cut for the wagons at the first sign of attack." Dallas wheeled his mount and slanted off into the barren ridges and rocky mesas on the southern side of the road, a wiry whipthong figure in the saddle.

Montrill signaled Crater's rear guard to close up a bit, then unslung his field-glasses and swept the arid chopped-up countryside in all directions. No sight of the Apaches from here, other than vague intermittent smoke puffs against the northern horizon. If Jim Raven was here, he could probably read that, or guess what they were communicating, Montrill thought. . . . No indication of relief from the west either. They should have met us by noon, and here the afternoon's half gone or better. Ashley wouldn't be this late; neither would Shaddock. It must be Herrold leading the patrol. Herrold no doubt had spotted a stray buck or two and gone sky-hooting off on the chase. Herrold acted as though he wanted personally to run down and kill every Indian in the territory. Commendable spirit, but it didn't make for tactical efficiency or operational unity.

It would be Herrold, of course. He had requested this assignment that Montrill was on. Cris wanted every mission that came up, the tougher the better, as if all he thought of was wiping out and making up for the tragic mistakes of his father and brother. No wonder Cris Herrold was like a man obsessed, lost in the grip of a strange madness. Montrill shook his head sorrowfully, hair glinting bronze in the sun.

Nearing the Cherokee Valley, they passed homesteads and small ranches that were abandoned or burned down, and Teresa Thurston realized that conditions had changed here during her absence. The Apaches were really up now, the country in a state of full-scale war. She began to comprehend the tension that rode with Montrill and his men.

The sun was dipping toward the westerly Osages, the shadows lengthening on the blistered earth, when Montrill halted for another rest period. If the Indians attacked it would come before nightfall, and Montrill had been searching for a defensible position. A sandstone butte loomed north of the trail here, and beneath an overhanging ledge was a recessed area large enough for wagons, mules and horses, sheltered by huge boulders and mounds of shale, screened with mesquite and catclaw clumps, creosote brush and prickly pear. A place he had noted previously as the best spot to fort up in for miles along this road.

Teresa Thurston climbed down from her wagon seat and walked to where Montrill was swabbing out the alkali-inflamed nostrils of his big bay gelding with a cloth wet from his canteen. "What has happened here, Rick, to make the Apaches so strong and brave? In the past they'd hesitate to attack an army detail openly."

"Not any more," Montrill said. "The Chiricahuas have come up with a chief called Hatchese, and the young bucks of other tribes are flocking to him. A leader in the tradition of Cochise and Geronimo, even more ruthless and daring, a natural-born strategist. Your father says Hatchese would have made a great commander of cavalry."

Teresa stood close, staring up at him with arch studied gravity. In spite of her willowy slimness, she had a strong curved fullness of breast and hip, as provocative and disturbingly feminine as the scent she wore. A moment ago Tess had been all army, and Montrill had been able to talk freely and easily with her that way. Now she was all woman, flaunting her sex and her charms, and he turned away, saying:

"I think we'll crawl into that hole in the wall and wait for darkness, or that overdue detachment from the fort."

Piqued again, the girl caught at his sweaty, long-muscled arm. "Even with things as they are, Rick, I am glad to be back here."

"You may change your mind about that in

the next hour, Tess."

She let go of his arm. "You can't frighten me, Mr. Montrill."

"I'm not trying to," he said. "Pardon me now; I've got some figuring to do."

Tess Thurston flounced away, golden head high and disdainful, and Montrill was aware of the troopers looking hungrily after her lissome rounded figure with its swaying, seductive stride. That girl needs to be roughed up and shaken down some, he thought with anger. She's dynamite amongst men who have almost forgotten what a white woman looks and feels and smells like. The Old Man never should have brought her back to Burnside.

Such things did not bother Montrill so much as they once had. With the years he had learned to discipline his appetites, control his emotions, and not yearn for the unattainable. Also, he had the companionship of Anita Raven to ease some of that normal need for women. But Montrill was stirred more than he would have admitted by the flagrant femininity of Teresa Thurston, and he knew that her presence was torture to the lonely starved men in the ranks.

Montrill called up the rear guard, and spoke with unaccustomed sharpness. "Dal-

22

las, Flint, bring in the flankers! Teamsters, drive in under that overhang there. Get the wagons in as far as possible. Crater, you and your boys clear the way. The rest of you men lend a hand with the wagons, and then prepare the place for defensive action."

The hooded freighters were parked in under the high broad outthrust of red rock, the horses picketed at the rear, and the soldiers at work improving the natural barricade at the mouth, when gunfire burst out on Seaver's flank in the north. Montrill had rolled and lighted a cigarette, and was standing long and limber at the roadside with a carbine in the crook of his arm. Waiting, suddenly stark and tense, watching for the flankers, Montrill drew hard on the cigarette and prayed silently, while the wind-torn sounds of shooting crackled and echoed along corridors of stone. *Come on, boys. Get in here fast. Once we're split up they'll overrun us all. We estimated about fifty braves, and maybe more. . . . Bring 'em back here, Seav; don't stop to fight! . . . Where the devil is Herrold with that blasted detail from the post?*

Dallas returned with Dunleavy's party on the gallop. Montrill held them waiting in the saddle while he mounted his bay. If Seaver was cut off, they'd have to go out there and break him loose. . . . The drumming clatter of shod hoofs reached them through the vicious whanging of rifles, and Montrill herded the others into the lofty open cavern as Seaver's crew cleared a low ridge and thundered toward the trail. Counting anxiously, Montrill sighed with relief to find nobody missing.

They were all under cover at the base of that butte, the place steaming with the sweat of horses and men, when the Indians fanned out along the barren slope and opened fire. Montrill let his men lash back with two rapid rounds, to indicate the firepower he had available, and then told them to hold it. The warriors, scattering for the sparse shelter out there, had a couple hundred yards of fairly open terrain to cross if they chose to try a frontal assault. At times the Apaches did yield to such suicidal impulses, but more rarely since Hatchese had assumed command.

They were dismounting, Montrill decided, to work their way forward on foot. With a lack of cover on that sunbaked slope and the kind of sharpshooters Montrill had behind the Winchester repeaters, that maneuver could become nearly as suicidal as a direct mounted charge. . . . The sinuous coppery bodies came snaking and slithering

24

on, utilizing every boulder and depression, pitahaya and sahuaro cactus column, each cluster of mescal, chaparral and ocotillo. Montrill passed the word to fire at will, and went to work with his own carbine. Flame stabbed out all along the barrier, as the Winchesters began to blast with steady deep-toned authority, ringing and beautiful in the military ear.

Dust spurts blossomed on the sandy incline, and here and there Indians screamed and threshed in pain, stiffened out on the reddish soil or jerked and fled in panic, the .44's still searching and raking and knocking down the half-naked, clay-daubed brown forms. The retreat was general now, but some of the bucks were still blazing away at the foot of that cliff. In the makeshift redoubt, the primary danger was from ricochets, as the bullets snarled and screeched off rock surfaces, showering the defenders with stone dust and splinters. The powder fumes thickened, acrid and choking, while the horses and mules snorted and stomped and whickered.

On the firing line the veterans might have been at target practice, commenting in dry profane disgust on their misses, calmly approving their hits, and chiding one another with rough sarcasm from time to time.

Forgetting the presence of the young lady they had been only too aware of a few minutes ago, their language was uninhibited and anything but elegant. Montrill, smiling grimly to himself, had no intention of reprimanding them. It might do the major's daughter good, although he doubted if she overheard any of it.

Teresa Thurston, stretched flat beneath a wagon at the rear of the reeking stronghold, heard nothing but the shattering roar of rifle fire and the awesome shriek of ricocheting lead. With her eyes shut tight most of the time, she saw only the pulsating blankness of the lids. When they did flick open momentarily, Tess focused them on the lithe kneeling figure of Rick Montrill, and somehow those glimpses were reassuring and comforting, made her feel slightly better.

The shooting tapered off gradually, dying out at last, and Tess opened her eyes to the sting of powdersmoke and alkali dust. Nobody seemed to be wounded, or even worried. Men were chatting casually as they reloaded, rinsed their mouths sparingly, lit up cigarettes and pipes or bit off fresh chews, teeth flashing white in blackened faces as they grinned. Montrill alone was somber and thoughtful, the burden of command bearing down on him. As if feeling

Teresa's gaze on him, he turned and looked down at her with a slow absent smile.

"All right, Tess? Nothing to worry about. They'll never get in here."

"But how will we get out, Rick?"

"That's the problem," Montrill confessed. "It should be solved when the reinforcements from Burnside arrive. They'll pry these Apaches off our necks, Tess."

"But there must be hundreds of Indians!"

Montrill shook his sandy head. "Only about fifty. Less than that now, I think."

The blood-red sphere of the sun was almost rimming the Osage ramparts, with gray and lavender shadows spreading and darkening to blue and purple on the raw wild landscape. The attack was in motion once more, slick swift forms flitting downgrade at the butte, orange muzzle-lights flaring back and forth like lightning, when the relief force struck the Apaches from behind. A reckless headlong cavalry charge, with the brassy blare of a trumpet shrilling through the hoofbeats and gunfire, pistols spurting and sabers slashing from horseback. The blue uniforms and yellow-striped trousers were a welcome sight.

Montrill knew it was Herrold before he could identify any of the hurtling riders. They smashed through the Indian horseholders on the ridge top, scattering and spilling ponies and braves in every direction, and came sweeping down the long uneven slope with guns aflame and sabers aglitter, riding over and through the unmounted warriors, killing some and driving all others into frantic flight. Dust stormed up high and red-hued in the light of the setting sun, and the cavalry came on in a thunderous, unstoppable torrent.

It was a stirring, thrilling spectacle in the desert dusk, lifting the heart, chilling the spine, and catching at the throat. A scene that Montrill would never forget. He felt like applauding, even while he questioned the tactics, and some of his troopers were cheering spontaneously. Don't be too critical now, Montrill advised himself in silence. It's easy to second-guess, but how would you have done it? . . . Showiness could not be condemned too much, when it was thoroughly effective and didn't cost lives.

Montrill found that Tess Thurston was standing beside him, clutching his arm and watching with wide fascinated eyes. "Isn't that wonderful?" she cried. "Isn't that marvelous? I never saw anything like it! It's Cris Herrold, isn't it?"

It was Crispin Herrold all right, intense and darkly handsome on his lathered blowing horse, pulling up before the breastworks in a boiling billow of dust. Behind him on the darkening slope it was all over, only the dead and wounded Apaches and ponies left strewn there. Herrold had some good hand-picked men with him too, Montrill observed. Sergeant Kirk, Corporals McCord and Shiller, Thackston, Vermilya, Detwiller, Cantey, Ginter, Ullrich, and other fine campaigners.

"Sorry to be late, Montrill. Unavoidably detained en route." There was a tinge of irony in Herrold's clear cultured tones. "We'll be getting after the stragglers now."

"There'll be no pursuit," Montrill said, stepping over the barricade with his carbine, a weapon that Herrold deemed unfit for officers.

Herrold paused on the verge of giving the order and stared haughtily down at the tall man on foot. "I command this column!"

"True. But I am in charge of the wagon train." Montrill's voice was quiet and even.

"You forget, sir, that I rank you!" Herrold said with scorn.

Montrill was silent, letting those words hang there in the stillness, sounding childish, cheap and unbecoming to an officer. Every man present knew that Montrill had been a Confederate captain at twenty-one, and now had eight years of service on this Southwest frontier, while Herrold was but two years out of West Point.

"True again," Montrill said finally. "But not on this mission. Our primary objective is to get these wagons to Burnside."

"I have orders to contact the enemy whenever possible," Herrold insisted sullenly, realizing the error of pulling his rank on a veteran like Montrill.

"You will not find the enemy in the darkness that's coming," Montrill said gently. "And you have wounded men in the ranks. We'll attend to them, Cris, while you see if there are any Indians out there who might be made to talk. . . . We'll eat here and continue the march after moonrise."

Herrold was furious, still wanting to argue but aware of the futility of it, and after bowing gracefully to Tess Thurston he named the troopers to follow him and led them back the way they had come, the girl watching him with eyes and face aglow.

The sun was gone, light lingering in the sky while dusk flooded the earth with desert suddenness, blue and cool and a blessed relief after the wicked glaring heat. The wounds were slight and superficial. Ginter had been raked by a lance, McCord's scalp was furrowed by a bullet, and a thrown hatchet had gashed Thackston's hip. Vermilya and O'Doul had received flesh wounds in arm and leg respectively. . . . Crispin Herrold had been lucky again, incredibly lucky. Montrill saw now how reckless, unnecessary and foolhardy that charge had been. A matter of inches, and five dead cavalrymen might have been sprawled on that rocky slope.

Old Seaver was grumbling as he helped dress the injuries. "The spit-and-polish squirt ranks *him!* Him who was Jeb Stuart's captain eleven years back. Ain't that the army for you though? Gawd in the foothills, with no cavalry in support!"

CHAPTER III

The following afternoon brought into view landmarks that Teresa Thurston recognized as being near the plateau on which Fort Burnside stood at the northern end of the Cherokee Valley. With the Mojave Desert farther behind the rumbling wagons, vegetation was changing, mesquite, nopal and Spanish bayonet giving way to sage and bunchgrass, the cactus and paloverde yielding to scrub oak, cedar and jack pine. Creeks that would be bone-dry later in the summer were flowing to join the Cherokee River, lined with willows and cottonwoods.

Straight ahead loomed the spired magnificence of Cathedral Rocks, amber and crimson in the brassy sunlight, and just south of them was the dark purplish bulk of Blue Mesa. Far to the north and west ranged the towering Osage Mountains, tier on massive serrated tier, and somewhere in that wilderness of pine slopes and craggy peaks lay the headquarters of Hatchese.

Tess Thurston was weary of this journey, exhausted from the pitiless heat, but she still made a brave show of vivacity when the eyes of the men were upon her. Last night when they made camp, she had strolled apart with Cris Herrold, stricken once more by his keen flawless beauty, touched by his proud loneliness. The troopers didn't like him, of course. He was too much of a gentleman, too fine and sensitive and aristocratic for this raw brutal existence.

It had been romantic in the moonlight, with Herrold slender and straight as a lance at her side and young Cantey's rich tenor voice raised in song from a campfire. And more than romantic when Cris held and kissed her. . . . Yet Crispin Herrold was not a comfortable person to be with, quite the contrary. Something was always fretting and nagging at his mind, fuming and seething inside him, goading and driving and never letting him relax or rest.

On the march today Herrold had been restless, impatient, irritated beyond reason by the slow dragging progress of the freighters, bored with plodding dullness and inactivity. There was no patience in the boy, he was too keyed up and intense, and if he didn't change he would not last long in this

Indian warfare. Something was bound to snap and break, and Cris Herrold would either be dead or disgraced. That charge yesterday had thrilled her to the core, but in sober retrospect Teresa was enough of a soldier to discern the tactical error in it. Cris could have driven off those Apaches without risking his entire force. Montrill would have done it with less show and speed, but a great deal more safeness and security.

This afternoon when Indian fires were sighted north of Cathedral Rocks, Herrold had wheedled Montrill into sending him out with a small scouting party. It was against Montrill's better judgment, but Herrold reiterated his plea that Major Thurston had instructed him to contact the enemy at every opportunity. With the fort not too far away now, Montrill had finally acquiesced, including Seaver and Dunleavy in the detachment as dual curbs on Herrold's rashness. Since yesterday's rout the Apaches had ceased hounding the wagon train, apparently not even trailing it at a distance.

On his own again, freed from the depressing drag and grind of the cumbersome wagons, as well as from Montrill's easy but inflexible authority, Herrold felt like himself once more, anticipating action, as near to happiness as he was likely to get in this pattern of life. He understood why Dunleavy and Seaver were along, knew that they despised him, but Herrold refused to be troubled to any extent by a pair of ancient worn-out noncoms. They were regular army; they'd take orders from a superior, regardless of what they thought of him or his commands.

Heading the short double file of horsemen, Herrold was tall, erect and graceful in the saddle, scornful of the hatred he could feel at his back. Butcher Boy was one of the many things they called him in the barracks. Crispin Herrold bore no resemblance to a butcher. He was well-built in a spare wiry fashion, the clean lines of blood and breeding evident in his figure as in his face. He was strikingly handsome, except for a certain tautness about the mouth, the hint of strain around his intense dark eyes. His features were straight and clear, finely chiseled, with a sharpness to the bones of cheek, jaw and chin. Crisp black hair curled under the campaign hat on his high well-shaped head. Even after two days of hard riding and fighting, Herrold had an innate elegance that transcended the sun-bleached, sweat-soaked, battle-grimed uniform.

Underneath his rather superior and arrogant manner, Herrold was a curious mixture of sensitivity and audacious strength, shyness and pride, gentility and driving force. Few people were aware of the milder qualities in him. But rarely, and then only to women, did Herrold reveal the gentler side of his complex nature.

He glanced back along the line and caught the cold slit-eyed scrutiny of Seaver and Dunleavy, the ten privates behind them, and the impact of feeling from the column was like a whiplash across Herrold's face. They'd like to see me dead and scalped, slow-roasted over an Apache fire perhaps, he thought. They blame me for every man that died under my father and my brother, along with the ones I've lost. . . . But they won't see me dead, damn their stupid souls! I'll outlive all of them. I've got to. I have so much more to live for.

In back of the lieutenant, Dunleavy turned his homely red face toward the other sergeant, heavy underslung jaws jutting beneath his low-pulled hatbrim. "The kid'll try to get us all killed off, Seav."

"Sure, and what do you expect, Dunny?" Seaver's seamed leathery face crinkled to the faded blue eyes with his grin. "He's a Herrold, ain't he? One way or another the

Herrolds always built up the casualty lists."

Dunleavy snorted. "What happened to his brother Derrick could happen to him one of these days."

"He keeps on the rate he's goin', it won't have to," said Seaver. "This boy'll write his own epitaph."

"In our blood," Dunleavy added dryly. "You think he knows about brother Dirk?"

"What he don't know he can mighty easy guess."

"It don't scare him none."

Seaver shook his graying head. "One thing you got to hand the kid, he's got guts."

Behind them Cantey was singing, *My Darling Clementine,* with Detwiller and Flynn coming in on the chorus, Kazmaier and Toneff laughing and shouting.

Herrold turned contemptuously in his saddle. "Quiet back there! You sergeants should know better than that. Dress those ranks! Straighten those hats! Sit your saddles like cavalrymen. Try to look something like soldiers!" They'd never learn, he thought. Dignity, self-respect, things like the hat being a uniform, were lost on them. They went to war like drunken bandits, or like Montrill's Confederate guerrillas perhaps. No sense of propriety or responsibility or tradition.

■ ■ ■ ■

Well north of Cathedral Rocks they moved into a long broad canyon, its walls broken irregularly by the branching off of smaller gulches and barrancas. Smoke signals were no longer visible, but Herrold had the direction fixed in his mind. Dunleavy, Seaver, and some of the other old campaigners were growing uneasy. They were already too far from the wagons, and in the command of a young madman who would never turn back, once he sighted the enemy. That had caused the delay yesterday: Herrold's playing tag with some of Hatchese's scouts. And it could have been disastrous to the wagon train and its escort and the major's daughter. Seaver shuddered to think of all those new Winchesters with ammunition in the hands of the Apaches. Why, they'd attack Burnside and wipe out the whole garrison, and then run wild over Arizona Territory.

Seaver moved up beside the lieutenant. "With due respect, sir, I believe we ought to turn back."

"There are Indians ahead."

"I know, sir. Just tryin' to lead us on."

"Any band we run into might take us to Hatchese," said Herrold.

"Not in this low country — sir."

"I command here, Seaver. We're going on."

Seaver dropped back without another word, chewing harder on his tobacco. The small Apache party was in plain view now, retreating before them along this main canyon. Seaver thought: They'll duck into a side alley pretty soon, and this fool will take us in after them. Then hell will bust loose all around us. . . . He saw it, as if he had lived through it before. And it started happening, exactly as he had foreseen.

The Indians vanished into a breach in the wall on their left, and Herrold led them forward at the gallop, reining up at the mouth of that diverging canyon. It was narrow, crooked, steep-walled, cluttered with boulders and talus drifts, shrouded with thickets of catclaw and cholla, hummocks of mescal, tangled groves of mesquite and paloverde — a perfect trap. Herrold looked at his noncoms, and both shook their heads. He glanced at the enlisted men, who sat motionless and silent.

"Well, what do you say?" asked Herrold, black eyes burning at the two sergeants, relishing this moment in some perverse way.

"It's no good, sir," Seaver said.

"There aren't enough of them to stand

and fight," declared Herrold.

"May be more of 'em in there," muttered Dunleavy.

Herrold laughed. "They won't risk a fight — after yesterday."

Seaver regarded him with honest surprise. "They've been hit a lot harder'n that, and come back fightin'."

"We'll go in and see," Herrold decided, driven by something stronger than himself, irked by the opposition and reluctance in the ranks. "Seaver and Dunleavy out with two flankers each. The rest by twos, march!"

So they went in, and to Seaver, moving out on the right flank with Detwiller and Ax Hendree, it was like a nightmare that he had dreamed before. Dunny's right, he thought. This kid's asking for the same thing his brother got. Be a blessing if the Apaches get him before that can happen. . . . Their quarry was still in sight, dangling like live bait in retreat, but Seaver was scanning the jagged wall and waiting for the slugs to smash him out of the leather, the burst of sound against his eardrums. Nothing to be seen on either wall, but they were there all right; Seaver could smell them and feel them. He had tasted fear many times, but never so strong and rancid. Because this was all pointless, foolish, and without meaning or worth.

It came with such shocking suddenness there was no reality. One instant all was quiet; the next, earth and sky seemed to explode into flame and roaring sound. Sheets of fire sprang from the ledges, showers of lances and arrows rained down with the lead, beating the brush, chipping boulders, and churning the canyon floor into smoking chaos.

Detwiller gasped and fell from the saddle, a lance driven clear through his body from right breast to left hip. Seaver and Hendree blasted that lance-thrower off the rock wall, and then there was nothing else to shoot at except muzzle flashes that seemed to jet from solid stone. Detwiller was done for, and Seaver shouted, "Ride for it, Ox!" and they wheeled their mounts back toward the central group. Glancing back, Seaver saw red-brown forms dropping around Detwiller, and heard him scream as they scalped and chopped at him with tomahawks. He and Ox emptied their carbines, downing some of those bucks.

Out in the middle, Flynn and Kazmaier with their horses had gone thrashing down under that scourging, withering crossfire, and the wonder was that any of them had survived it. On the left wing, Toneff's horse had been shot in under him as they started to pull back, and three howling half-stripped warriors were on top of Toneff immediately, with knives and hatchets slashing. Those three died under the carbines of Dunleavy and Emmett, but that was all they could do and it was too late for Toneff.

Reunited in the center, the nine survivors fanned out and fled wildly for the mouth of that flaming corridor, under a hail of bullets and arrows, horses and riders flattened out in full straining speed. Seaver half-expected to collide with another enemy force at the entrance, but no such thing occurred, and somehow they cleared that tortuous passage and swept back down the main canyon toward Cathedral Rocks. Nine of them still alive on horses that could still run, and not one of them able to believe it as yet.

But one thing they did know well, too well. Back there in that hideous labyrinth, four good men of the Third lay lifeless, dead and mutilated beyond any semblance of humanity by now. Detwiller and Toneff, Flynn and Kazmaier. . . . For no sane reason or purpose, four lives had been thrown away. And looking at the officer responsible, it was all Seaver and others could do to keep from drawing and shooting him down.

"It ain't often," grated Dunleavy, "that

we're beat so bad we can't pick up our own dead."

"If them Indians could hit anythin' with a rifle, not a single one of us would of got outa there," Seaver said, spitting viciously. "I still don't see how they missed at that range."

"They'll chop 'em to pieces back there," mumbled the stocky Emmett, his broad sweat-varnished face haunted.

"They're dead!" Herrold cut in bitterly. "They're beyond suffering now."

Seaver stared at him with cold implacable hatred. Dunleavy said heavily: "Ain't much question about that, Lieutenant."

Herrold pushed on ahead, hating himself now, wishing one of those bullets had found him in that shot-torn arroyo. He'd been wrong, horribly wrong. The Butcher Boy had led four more to the slaughter. Dread and revulsion filled him at the prospect of facing Montrill and Major Thurston and the whole garrison. Herrold shook his head desperately, fiercely, but there was no getting away from it. He could still see Flynn and Kazmaier going down riddled, and those brown-skinned bodies settling like vultures upon Toneff. He could still hear Detwiller screaming through the gunfire and the smoke-blued yellow dust. Those things would be with him as long as Herrold lived. . . . Half an hour ago he had felt unconquerable and immortal. Now death seemed almost welcome, the only way out for him.

There was no pursuit. The Apaches had been so sure of their prey that they were unprepared to follow up, their ponies gathered at some distance to guarantee surprise in the ambuscade. The trap had been set to perfection, the massacre should have been total. . . . Would have been but for the Grace of God, a freak of fortune, or whatever one chose to term it.

"They was sure primed and set for us," growled big Ox Hendree. "They must know our officers. Never would of pulled one like that on Monty."

"Sure, they know the officers," Seaver said. "Know some of us dog soldiers, for that matter. Ought to; we been out here long enough."

"Indians all look alike to me," said young Cantey.

"The only time they look good is dead," muttered Hendree.

Old Seaver spoke gravely, thoughtfully. "They was here first, Ox. They've got somethin' to fight for. This was their country."

"You turnin' Injun-lover, Sarge?" jeered

Hendree.

"Not hardly, but right is right," Seaver insisted gently. "I got most of this from Monty. Room enough for whites and reds both here. Wouldn't be no trouble if chiefs like Geronimo, Nana, Chatto, and Hatchese didn't come along like red Napoleons cravin' for power."

"But we got to put 'em down, ain't we, Seav?" asked Hendree.

"Pretty likely, Ox. It's the only way to get peace and open this land up for settlement."

It was too late to rejoin the main column, Herrold discovered with relief. The wagon train had crossed Skeleton Ridge, passed between Blue Mesa and Cathedral Rocks, traversed the sandy dunes and alkali flats, and was climbing the switchback road near the whitespumed falls in the Cherokee, to the high vast tabletop which held Fort Burnside and Forrester's Flying F spread. The Winchesters were safe, at any rate, the mission a success — except for Herrold's bullheaded blundering.

Keeping a slow pace, forming a sort of rear guard, Herrold brought his patrol across the bottoms in a twilight haze. Mounting toward the lofty rimrock, cleanly outlined against the fading colors of the western sky, Herrold could feel the hate like a solid thing on the back of his sunburnt neck and shoulders. At the top, the stockade of Burnside came into view, stretched on lower ground at the river bank. The wagons were already inside the gates, their dust pall hovering in the violet dusk. Teresa Thurston was home again — if you could call it that.

From the rim they could see the post within those weathered walls, its bleak imperfections softened by distance and twilight. The long pineboard barracks and mess halls, the wide stables, corrals and huddled outbuildings. Headquarters, severe and solid over the level parade, the boxlike adobes of officers' row, hospital, commissary, bakeshop, guardhouse, the flagless pole, its colors down for the night. . . . The familiar sight did not cause Herrold's heart to rise gladly, as it sometimes did on returning from a scout. He was far too miserable and apprehensive of the ordeal ahead.

It was dark when they filed through the gate into camp, and Herrold knew that evening mess was over and the men would be out watching this belated entry, counting the riders and finding four missing . . . "Well, he's done it again," they'd tell one another grimly. "He never brings back a full detail, not that Herrold. The Butcher Boy always kills off some of his command."

Turning the men over to Sergeant Seaver for dismissal and leaving his jaded mount with them, Herrold walked slowly and stiffly toward the larger 'dobe at the head of officers' row, hollow nausea in his stomach and the taste of acid in his throat. Major Thurston and Teresa stood together under the brush ramada, the major smoking a cigar, with one arm on his daughter's shoulders. The arm dropped when Herrold's boots struck the duckboards, and Tess slipped inside the house.

Herrold saluted and made his report, clear and concise, not sparing himself whatsoever. Thurston listened, the tired expression growing on his lined, sun-ruddy face. He was a short man, wide and solid and gaining weight in his fifties, with piercing dark eyes, graying hair, and a gray mustache. Herrold finished and Thurston examined his cigar, as if it had become abruptly distasteful.

"You admit to faulty judgment?" Thurston said. "It has been at fault before, and we cannot afford these mistakes. Losing four men here is like losing an entire troop in some campaigns, Herrold. Men like those four are irreplaceable on this frontier."

Herrold was silent, rigid as a ramrod, and

the major went on: "I'm relieving Mr. Barron as post adjutant. You will take over in his place."

Herrold winced involuntarily, then masked his fine features. "Yes, sir. Unless you'd prefer my resignation?"

Major Thurston regarded him stonily. "If we weren't short-handed I'd consider that, Herrold. As it is, I recommend that you withhold it. For the present, at least. It is no dishonor to serve as adjutant."

"But I'm a field officer, sir."

The generous mouth tightened under the gray mustache. "You will take over as adjutant tomorrow. Mr. Barron will instruct you for a day or so as to the routine and duties. That is all, Lieutenant."

"Yes, sir." Herrold saluted smartly, and turned down the row toward his own quarters. All at once, more than anything in the world, he needed the understanding sympathy and warm comfort of Anita Raven. Below his station, half-breed daughter of the post's chief Indian scout or not, she was the only one who could soothe Herrold in times like this. . . . But Montrill was more than likely to be with Anita. He was always rubbing horns with that easy going Rebel, Montrill.

Major Thurston, his cigar drawing nicely

again, stared thoughtfully after the tall proud figure of young Herrold, musing: Never should have sent the boy out here. Not to Burnside, not anywhere in this Territory. He tries too hard to live down his father and his brother, too damn hard altogether. It's like a triple burden on his back. Somewhere else Herrold might have been all right. . . . Thurston shuffled slowly back into the adobe.

Teresa looked up at him and frowned, quick to sense trouble. "What's the matter, Major?" She was blonde, young, brimming with vital life in the lamplight.

"Herrold lost four men this afternoon," Thurston said, chewing on the cigar.

"Oh, no!" she cried protestingly. "Oh, Dad. . . . Who were they?"

He named them slowly, each one taking its toll of grief.

"Why, last night they were singing," the girl murmured wonderingly. "With Cantey, around the campfire."

"Surprised and whipped so badly, they had to leave the bodies."

After an interval of silence, Teresa asked: "Dad, what are you going to do — to Cris Herrold?"

"Nothing much. Make him post adjutant, as of tomorrow."

"He'll never stand for that, Dad."

"It's that or nothing, Tess. We can't afford to lose men the way he loses them. Flynn was with me at the first Bull Run. Detwiller saved my life at Redstone Butte last year."

"What a shame!" sighed Teresa. "Cris is a fighter, but he'll never be a soldier, I guess."

Major Thurston wagged his gray head. "Not exactly, Tess. The boy *is* a soldier, but he's *not* an Indian fighter."

"You're juggling terms on me, Major," said the girl. "But I bow to your superior age, experience and wisdom."

Thurston smiled and brushed his gray mustache across the soft gleaming gold of her hair. "It's good to have you back, Tess. I've been lonesome here."

CHAPTER IV

Anita Raven kept house for her father Jim in a snug log cabin set in a far corner of the stockade beyond officers' row. Clean, comfortable, bright with Navajo rugs and drapes, it was the most pleasant and homelike place of the post. On his third night back Montrill had taken supper there, as he frequently did, preferring it to officers' mess in the Thurston adobe. After the meal Jim Raven had wandered off somewhere, pipe in teeth, leaving the dishes to his daughter and Montrill, who rather enjoyed this casual domesticity, although he never considered himself a particularly domestic man.

Now they sat together on the sparse dry grass before the house, watching the moon rise in full glory and change from orange to gold and then silver, as it climbed above the jagged barrier of distant mountain ranges. Last night there had been a dinner and reception for Teresa Thurston in the commanding officer's quarters, to which Anita Raven had not been invited. It wasn't very festive, with Herrold frozen in a remote silence which chilled the assemblage.

"Tess and I were pretty friendly once," Anita Raven remarked, with a trace of wistfulness.

"You're too attractive for that to last, Nita," said Montrill, smiling. "Tess likes to be the belle of the ball. The wives of Captain Jepson and Captain Trible don't offer much competition — but you would. It was a sorry gathering."

"Cris Herrold's taking it hard, isn't he?"

"It hit us all. That whole detail could have been wiped out."

"I know, Rick. I feel it, too. . . . But I can't help thinking of Cris. He's been close to breaking for quite a while. This might do it."

Montrill shrugged slightly, wondering again at her continued interest in Cris Herrold. "Maybe that's the best thing that could happen."

Anita Raven sighed. "Maybe, Rick. I don't know. . . ."

She did not flaunt her sex like Teresa Thurston, but it was there, strong and compelling, rousing the quick interest and desire of any man who was near her. Anita was simple and natural in manner, without artifice or guile, but her physical appeal was like a flame. As dark as Teresa was fair, Anita Raven had the rare vivid beauty that mixed blood sometimes creates. Jet black hair drawn back, smooth and shining, from the almost classic features. The clear gray eyes, her sole heritage from Jim, were startlingly light and luminous in the flawless dark skin of her face. Tall for a woman and superbly shaped, she had the supple effortless grace of an animal, and there was something wild and exotic about the girl.

Her Mexican mother must have been a real beauty, Montrill thought, for old Jim was gaunt and ugly as a timber wolf. Anita had been to school, in Western towns and on army posts, and she spoke in musical tones with only an odd inflection here and there, a faint intriguing accent. She was as intelligent, as much of a lady as the major's daughter. And more of a woman, Montrill concluded. Way too much woman for a kaydet like Herrold.

Lounging there beside her, broad shoulders against the logs, Montrill was long and limber and relaxed, big and loose-jointed, casual in his uniform and his easy ways, quiet and slow-talking. Power and grace were blended in his rangy frame and large fine-shaped hands. The lean rugged features were grave, almost somber in repose, but there was humor around the wide mouth and mild gray-green eyes, and Montrill was boyish when he smiled.

"You're so calm and easy and comfortable, Rick," said Anita, studying him in the moonlight. "Not like Crispin. . . . He has something in here driving him, driving him all the time." She touched her breast. "It won't let him rest, Rick. He is never happy."

"Not even with you, Nita?" drawled Montrill.

"Not all the way happy." Her black head gleamed as it turned.

"Who is?" Montrill asked whimsically. "Herrold could be perhaps. He has something that you women like."

"Maybe it's because he needs us. And you don't, Rick. You are — well, complete, I guess. You don't need anybody."

"But I do, Nita." He laughed softly. "That shows how little a woman's intuition tells her about a man."

"Not like Cris does."

Montrill grinned. "I am a little too old to arouse the mother instinct."

"You're never serious," she accused him. "And Cris is too serious. About the army and everything else."

"He was born into the army. That's one thing, I suppose."

"That should make it easier, better."

"Sometimes, but not always," Montrill said. "It can work the other way, too."

"Yes, of course," Anita agreed. "On account of his father and brother. Why do you stay in the army, Rick?"

He lifted his shoulders a trifle. "It's all I know, Nita. I kind of like it, being with men and horses and guns. And I don't like to work."

"But this is harder. The hardest kind of work there is."

"It's better though. For me, at least."

"But you aren't all military — like Cris."

"No, I'm not West Point," Montrill said. "Just a dog soldier, up from the ranks."

Anita Raven smiled, frankly and fondly. "I wish Cris was more like you, Rick."

"Then you wouldn't want him, Nita."

"I wouldn't say that, Rick. Everybody likes you."

Montrill shook his tawny head. "Not everybody, Nita. Enlisted men and horses, children and dogs maybe."

They were laughing lightly, shoulder to shoulder, when a long shadow fell slanting across them. Crispin Herrold, immaculate in his tailored uniform, brushed and polished to perfection, stood slim and straight over them, rigid and disapproving. "I hope I'm not intruding," he said, with stiff sarcasm.

"Cut it out, Cris," drawled Montrill. "Sit down and relax."

Herrold inspected the turf but remained erect and unrelaxed. "I understood I was to see you at this time, Anita."

"That's right, Cris."

"If it isn't too inconvenient, I prefer seeing you alone."

"Don't be unreasonable — and unpleasant, Cris," said Anita Raven. "Rick was invited here for supper. He knew you were coming later."

Herrold smiled with cool asperity. "If his invitation extends throughout the evening, I'll be glad to withdraw."

Montrill got up with indolent ease and dusted his trousers, the girl rising beside him. "That won't be necessary; I'm leaving," he said. "Thanks for the supper, Nita."

"You don't need to hurry, Rick," protested Anita.

"I've got some things to talk over with Jim. Good night, Nita." Montrill smiled at her and looked at Herrold, turning his head from side to side as if in pity.

Instant resentment flared in Herrold and

he stepped forward, hands jerking halfway up into fists, black eyes blazing and lips thinned tautly. They were nearly of a size, Montrill an inch taller than Herrold's six-foot height and somewhat heavier, but Herrold had youth on his side, and it increased his arrogance. With a contemptuous hand he waved toward officers' row in a gesture of dismissal.

Montrill stood slack and easy, long arms hanging carelessly at his sides. "You're jumpy, boy. And always asking for trouble. Some day you're going to get more of it than you bargain for."

"Any time you want it!" Herrold said harshly.

"Not here, not tonight. But you'll get it, Cris, if you keep on."

"Get out!"

Montrill smiled faintly. "I said I was leaving and I am. But not on your command, mister."

Herrold started for him, but Anita Raven stepped between them and caught his muscle-ridged arms. Montrill watched them for a moment, still smiling, and then turned away toward the parade ground.

"What's the matter with you, Crispin?" the girl demanded. "There was no call for this."

"I don't know; I'm sorry," Herrold mumbled, dropping his clenched hands, As the fingers opened out, he was suddenly loose and limp in her embrace. Anita held him, her voice gentle now.

"I know it's been hard, Cris. You've had a bad time."

He nodded dully. "Then to find him here!"

"Rick's nice. He'd be a good friend, Cris — if you'd let him."

"I don't want him," Herrold said. "I don't need friends. I don't want anybody — but you."

"But Rick could help you so much."

"Help me?" Herrold laughed scornfully. "I don't need any help, especially his. Why, he shouldn't even be an officer. Back East they'd break him in a minute."

"This isn't back East, Cris," she reminded him quietly.

"No, it certainly isn't!" There was disgust in Herrold's tone. "It's the ragged edge of civilization. The ranks are filled with rabble and riffraff, and there's scarcely a gentleman in officers' row."

"Cris, you know that isn't true," Anita Raven said. "You don't mean that at all."

"Why not? How many West Pointers are there on the staff?"

The girl drew away from him. "There are other gentlemen in the world. And what does West Point teach you about fighting Indians?"

Herrold looked at her in astonishment and despair. "You too?" he said brokenly. "Anita, I never thought you'd turn on me, too."

"I haven't, Cris. Nobody has. The trouble is you turn on the world, Crispin. You turn yourself inside out."

He melted again. "Sorry, Anita. Forgive me, Nita."

"Come and sit down," she murmured. "Let me hold you, Cris. You haven't been getting any sleep, I know. You're an awfully tired boy."

Resting against the cabin wall, Anita Raven pillowed his head on her lap. Gradually Herrold's face smoothed out and his eyes closed, as she soothingly caressed his fevered brow and curly dark hair, feeling the fury and tension ease out of him at last. Watching him tenderly, Anita thought: Why, he's just a little boy, hurt and lonely and sad — and very sweet.

Jim Raven returned and found them there, grimacing when he recognized Herrold in place of Montrill. Of all the soldiers in the fort, his daughter had to fall for this one. Well, maybe she'd come to her senses in time. How any woman could choose this punk kid over a man like Montrill was beyond him, but women were spooky, flighty critters, even the best of them. Take Nita's mother now, God rest her soul. She might have gone for the gold braid and brass, if he hadn't set her straight. Soft words and a hard hand, that's what held a woman. Montrill was too easy with Nita; Jim would have to prod him awake.

"Where's Monty?" he asked, shifting his chew of tobacco.

Anita nodded in the direction of the adobe houses. Herrold appeared to be sleeping, his handsome head cushioned on her lap.

"Reckon I'll drift over and see him." Jim Raven glanced at Herrold, spat expressively, and loped off in long silent strides, tall, slightly stooped, lean and lank, his scarred hawk-face weathered nearly black and his eyes like pale gray fire.

Jim had some news he'd been saving for Montrill, picked up on a lone scout while Monty was after that shipment of arms. If the information was authentic, they should be able to locate Hatchese's main camp, deep in the northwestern Osages. Now that they had enough Winchesters for the whole garrison, Thurston was more anxious than ever to engage Hatchese in a major and decisive battle. So far there'd been nothing but scouting forays, sniping duels, hit-and-run skirmishes, the Indians generally getting the best of it and disappearing before the cavalry could retaliate.

Stars swarmed overhead, the moon was a high white disk, and the limitless Arizona night dwarfed man to pinpoint insignificance. The sentry call resounded from post to post, and lights winked out around the quadrangle. A glance at the Big Dipper told Jim Raven it was time for taps, and he grinned as the running figures of some late drinkers broke from the sutler's for K barrack. There were still lights and minor activity about headquarters, the bakery and the stables. As Jim moved along the row, the slow mournful notes of taps ran across the parade and out over the plateau.

He found Montrill and Ashley in the 'dobe they shared, with glasses in hand and a bottle on the table between them. These were the only two officers at Burnside that Raven felt comfortable and at home with, the only ones he rated as real regular and natural men. The others put too much stock in military trappings, rank, insignia, and caste. Monty and Ash were men first and officers second.

Montrill hooked his toe around an empty

packing case and hauled it over to serve as an extra chair for the scout, while Ashley produced another glass and poured him a copious drink. Raven lifted it to them, swallowed with pleasure, and sighed in satisfaction. The three men were fully at ease together in the simple Spartan quarters. Ashley, much smaller that the others, was slight of stature and keen of feature, with friendly brown eyes and prematurely thinning brown hair. Sedate and subdued in repose, Ashley was a whiplash in action, smart and quick, wiry and tough, a good line officer.

"What's that good word, Jim?" inquired Montrill.

"You knew I had somethin', huh? Didn't wanta fret Nita with it, Monty," said Raven, in his deliberate brooding way. "I was out on my own when you was gone. Run into a little old Tonto I knew in the old days, done a favor for once. Gave me a line on where Hatchese's home camp is, way back in the Osages."

Both younger men were leaning forward now, alive with interest, and Jim Raven rambled on: "May not be the goods but it's worth a try. You know that break beyond Three Chiefs, high desert and stone chimney country? It's past there, up between

Castle Rock and The Brothers, near as I can figure from what the Tonto said."

"How come he'd talk, Jim?" asked Montrill.

"Don't like Hatchese. Claims Hatchese got three of his sons killed on the warpath."

"That's about where you always figured, Jim," mused Ashley.

Raven smiled. "That was just a hunch, Ash. This is a little more. Not much maybe, but some."

"Not enough to move full strength on," Montrill said thoughtfully. "A patrol first, to make sure and pull them out, with K and L in reserve, ready to hit them."

"Somethin' like that, Monty," agreed Raven.

They discussed it further over their drinks and cigars. When Jim Raven got ready to leave, he fixed his pale stare on Montrill. "One more thing, Monty, about Nita. You ain't playin' a strong enough hand there, son."

"Perhaps not. But I always let the girl call the play, Jim."

"You think I like to see her with that dressed-up tin soldier? That lad-dog dude of a Herrold?"

Montrill moved his bronze head negatively. "But I never liked to crowd them much."

"You musta missed out on a lot of stuff then, a whole helluva lot." Raven scowled and shook his long black hair, that was only a little flicked with gray.

"I suppose I have," Montrill smiled. "But what I got, Jim, was good, from the heart, without strings or reservations."

Raven grinned and gestured. "Reckon it was at that, Monty. 'Night, boys." He went out soundlessly, lanky and thin in his buckskins, the open-holstered Colts and a hunting knife sagging his shell belt.

"Some Jim," laughed Ashley, stubbing his cigar butt.

"He's quite a Raven all right," Montrill agreed with a fond smile.

CHAPTER V

For years the Apaches, under various fighting chiefs, had harassed southeastern Arizona along the San Pedro and Salt River, from the San Simon to the Huachucas, from the Gila to the Mexican border. With the rise of Hatchese the scene had shifted somewhat to the Cherokee Valley and the Osage Mountains, the storm breaking over the wild area guarded only by K and L troops of the Third Cavalry at Fort Burnside. B, the first company to occupy the post, had been decimated to the point where its survivors were utilized as replacements for K and L.

The climax was certain to come this summer. Hatchese, gaining steadily in strength with his Chiricahuas up from the Dragoons, Tontos down from the Mogollons, along with Coyotero and Aravaipa Apaches, was growing constantly bolder in his depredations against the settlers, increasingly contemptuous of the United States Army. Since early spring the raids had been more widespread and daring.

Prospectors' cabins and small ranches and homesteads were attacked and burned, stagecoaches and wagon trains were held up and cut to pieces, and cattle were run off from even the larger outfits, such as Forrester's Flying F near the fort. Striking with the suddenness of summer lightning, the Indians slashed in and out with fanatical hatred and murderous fury. Torturing, killing, burning, insane with the blood lust Hatchese had roused, pillaging and plundering in a berserk red reign of terror. . . . Buzzards flocked over the mutilated bodies of white men, women and children, and black smoke clouded up from the bloody shambles of wilderness homes.

Major Thurston and his junior officers aged by the day. One or two details were always on the trail, and the Apaches seemed forever in front of them but never within reach. Unseen snipers picked off a trooper here and there, but the cavalrymen seldom got a fair shot at the enemy. It was frustrating, maddening, nerve-rending work for the patrols from Burnside. There was always the feeling that Hatchese and his bucks were laughing at the soldiers, gloating over their helplessness.

Rumor reached the post that Hatchese had boasted he would sweep the Cherokee clean. "If this keeps on, gentlemen," Major Thurston solemnly told his staff, "he will do precisely that, and before autumn."

The officers, as well as the rank-and-file, felt their repeated failures deeply, but groped in vain for solutions to the problem. It was like pursuing phantoms in the wilderness. This arid jigsaw country was ideal for Apache tactics. Broken by sharp ridges, rocky buttes and wooded hills. Criss-crossed with mazes of crooked canyons and dry washes. Fringed in mesquite and catclaw clumps, hummocks of mescal and bayonet bush. Scattered with boulders, talus debris and pitahaya columns. . . . Stripped to breech-clouts and moccasins on their swift sure-footed ponies, the warriors were like fleeting brown shadows that melted away in the scorching air.

The troopers, sweltering in blue woolen uniforms and weighted down with thirty or forty pounds of equipment, were hopelessly handicapped in this killing heat. Embittered by failure, rankled with a sense of futility, every man in Burnside longed and prayed and cursed for the chance of meeting Hatchese and his braves in head-on combat.

But it did not look as if the opportunity would ever come — until Jim Raven produced a fresh scrap of evidence that revived waning hopes. But it was only hearsay, the word of an ancient Tonto, and most of the officers were frankly skeptical.

"I ain't passin' it off as gospel truth," Raven grumbled.

"We understand that, Jim," said Major Thurston, glaring from his headquarters desk at the officers who were exchanging ironical looks. "What's your opinion on putting this information to use?" He wondered just how many average lieutenants a scout like Raven was worth, in this kind of warfare. The figure, if honestly arrived at, would not credit the Military Academy.

"Well, you'll never get in there and catch 'em with a whole column, Major," said Jim Raven. "Scouted that section before, and they just fade and scatter. Two or three men from a detail might slip in and hang onto their tail. Spot the main bunch for you to strike at, maybe."

"I've considered that, Jim. But it would be virtually suicide for those two or three men."

Raven hunched his high bony shoulders. "Bound to be some loss, Major. Better lose two or three than twenty or thirty."

"True enough," Thurston assented. "But I

think we'll try one more regular scouting expedition to that area first. Any comments or suggestions, gentlemen?" He surveyed the officers seated about his office.

Captain Jepson was stolid, indifferent, pipe clamped in his square heavy-jowled face. Captain Trible shifted nervously, recrossed his spindling legs, scratched at his thin cheek and handlebar mustache. Herrold stared haughtily into space, aristocratic features set in a cold superior mask. Only Montrill and Ashley seemed easy, quietly alert and thoughtful.

Lieutenant Shaddock leaned forward, brawny arms on solid knees, large shaggy head thrusting on the bull-neck. "Sir, I'd put the whole force out after them this time!"

"Not yet, Mr. Shaddock. Not until we have a definite objective and plan of procedure."

Ray Barron, recently post adjutant, stirred his broad bulk and cocked his carefully pomaded head. "I'd like to request, sir, that I be included in this scouting detail." His sleek head and suave manner belied the bold ruthless aspect of his Roman-nosed, thin-lipped face.

"I'm sorry, Mr. Barron," said Thurston. "This particular mission requires officers with more experience in the field. But your turn will come, I assure you. Anything else, gentlemen?"

Montrill looked up and spoke, low and even. "If the occasion should arise on this scout, sir, I suggest that the officer in command be permitted to exercise his own judgment about putting Jim's plan into effect."

"You have a point there, Mr. Montrill, and I'll think it over. If the opportunity is right, it should not be wasted. Weeks or months might pass before another came — if another ever did come." Major Thurston cleared his throat, sensing the disapproval of his staff, the jealous feeling that Montrill and Ashley were favored here, along with Jim Raven. But it didn't matter. He had to use the best he had, and that's what he was doing. . . . Thurston continued with firm authority:

"Meanwhile Mr. Montrill and Mr. Ashley will head a detachment of twenty-five, selected from either troop. And Jim Raven will accompany them. If you three will remain now, the rest of you gentlemen are excused."

The conference over, Crispin Herrold walked out without looking at anyone and crossed the hall to his adjutant's office, shutting the door behind him with emphasis, as Barron made a tentative move toward following him. Standing by the front windows, Herrold watched his fellow officers step outside of headquarters and pause in the shade. A water-cart was sprinkling down the sun-dazzled parade, but one end dried to powdery dust before the other was wet. Amber dust geysered from the corrals, where Tex Dallas and other expert riders were breaking new mounts. A ringing clamor of steel hammering steel sounded from the blacksmith shop. In the barracks' shade, Seaver, Kirk, Dunleavy, and other sergeants were instructing groups in the handling of the new Winchester repeater. Freight wagons were being unloaded at the commissary and the sutler's store. At the far end of officers' row, Teresa Thurston strolled out to make a belated visit to the Raven cabin.

Herrold's dark gaze returned to his associates on the plank veranda. Look at that staff, he thought with derision. Except for Barron, they might have bought those uniforms in a secondhand sale or a pawn shop. Jepson and Trible were good men once, but had outlived their usefulness. Jepson, fat and sloppy, had just stopped caring.

A dozen years with a nagging wife had left the scrawny Trible neurotic.

Look at the hulking Shaddock, head down and boots pawing the boards in anger, bull-like in everything he did. A man without fear, but also without brains. And Barron, acting angry and thwarted himself, was nothing but an arm-chair officer, an efficiency model in paper work. What a hell of a way to run an army, Herrold thought. Why didn't they get rid of the deadwood, give the young and able men a chance to prove themselves and rise in the ranks? . . . Then it occurred to him that the Old Man was doing exactly that in this instance, but he had chosen Montrill and Ashley, and consigned Herrold to the deadwood. And on performance and record to date, Herrold couldn't justly blame him.

At times Cris Herrold wished he had never seen West Point nor the U. S. Cavalry, and was positive he should have followed any career but the military. The unfortunate lives of his own father and brother should have been enough to warn him off, but when things went wrong with them Crispin was already at the Point. He had seen in their downfalls a double challenge to himself, Herrold realized, and with youthful idealism he had dedicated his life to wiping out the disgrace they had brought on the family name.

After the War of the Rebellion when the army first moved into Arizona Territory, his father, Colonel Justin Herrold, had been stationed at Burnside as second-in-command. A fiery and fearless leader, an ambitious and forward-driving man, Justin Herrold had a splendid war record under Sherman and was widely known as Hellfire Herrold. But his dashing tactics met with less success in the West, and Justin was too proud and stubborn to change methods. He was evidently afflicted with some of the same rashness that made Custer so colorful and unpredictable.

On the trail of Cochise, said to be an uncle of this Hatchese, Colonel Justin Herrold had led a company of cavalry far to the south along the Querhada River, and into a trap where they were slaughtered — but not quite to the last man. A handful of survivors remained when the relief came up. Justin Herrold was unfortunate enough to be one of them. Seaver, a private at that time, was another. And Kazmaier had lived through that massacre, to die six years later under Justin Herrold's second son in a nameless canyon north of Cathedral Rocks.

It was disclosed that Justin Herrold had

disobeyed orders in pursuing Cochise that far. He was court-martialed and eventually cashiered from the service, to die soon afterward, a lonely, crushed and heartbroken man. His wife followed him almost immediately to the grave, and the two boys were left alone.

Crispin was then a plebe at the Military Academy, and Derrick was in his final year there. Upon being graduated and commissioned into the army, the elder brother Dirk was ordered to Arizona and wound up at Burnside, an evidence of the irony of fate and the perverse obtuseness of military procedure.

Under the black and heavy shadow of that tragedy on the Querhada, the brand of the name he bore, Derrick quite naturally bent over backward to avoid anything that bordered even remotely on rashness. The boy was so ultra-conservative, in fact, that his courage came to be questioned. It was said that Dirk Herrold refused to fight, unless the Apaches attacked him and there was no place to run or hide. Officers with insight and understanding, such as Major Thurston, comprehended the reasons behind this and requested a transfer for Derrick, but higher authority was obdurate. So he stayed on at Burnside, until the inevitable climax.

Young Cris Herrold, living in isolation and dread at the Point, had been so sure that something of this nature would happen, he was scarcely surprised when the news reached the Hudson. He made his vow then, setting the unalterable course of his life.

It had occurred when Derrick Herrold sat back in the scrubby sand hills over the Aravaipa and restrained his command of thirty, while Geronimo, with Hatchese as a sub-chief and an estimated band of one hundred braves, surrounded and butchered another detail of twenty troopers from Fort Burnside in the sun-seared valley below. The cavalrymen on the rimrock begged and pleaded, cursed and threatened, but Dirk Herrold would not order an attack.

"We can't save them; they're done for," he insisted. "We'd only be throwing away thirty more lives."

Rick Montrill, a sergeant along with Seaver then, was in that patrol on the hilltop, and his brother Lance was with the detachment down there at the creek. "They'll run if we hit them, Lieutenant," argued Rick. "They won't stop to see how many we are."

"They're dead already," Derrick said. "It's no use, Sergeant."

"We can break and scatter 'em. We've done it before!"

"Not against those odds. I can't risk it, Sergeant. This column is not expendable, for a cause already lost."

"Well, I am," Rick Montrill told him. "They're still fighting back, hang it all, and I'm going down!"

"You forget yourself, Sergeant," warned Dirk Herrold. "I'll put you under arrest!"

Some of them were either dead or dying on the river flats by then. The Apaches saw to it that several didn't die too quickly or easily, and the hideous screams floated up the hillside. . . . Montrill eyed the lieutenant with a look those men would never forget.

"My brother's down there," Rick Montrill said simply, swinging into the saddle and sliding his mount down the slope.

"I'm with you, Monty," called Seaver, dropping his horse over the rim.

Dunleavy and others started to follow, but Derrick Herrold had drawn his revolving pistol, and his voice checked them. "Hold up, you men, or I'll fire on you!"

Seaver hauled around and lifted his carbine, and below him Montrill whirled with Colt in hand, but a shot crashed out from somewhere before either of them or the officer could press a trigger. Smoke thinned along the rimrock, fading against the brassy molten sky, and Derrick Herrold swayed with bent head and keeled slowly from his saddle, dead before he struck the hot shale.

Looking downhill again, Montrill and Seaver saw that they were too late now. It was all over on the bank of the Aravaipa, all over but the howling and scalping and disfiguring of the dead.

Nothing for this detail to do but line out before the Indians swarmed after them. They returned to Burnside with an account of the massacre and Lieutenant Derrick Herrold's body tied across his horse. A detachment would be sent out to bury what was left of the others. There wouldn't be enough to bring home to the post cemetery. . . . Seaver and Montrill reported to the commanding officer.

"A sniper got the lieutenant, sir," Seaver said.

"Were you close enough to move in?" asked Major Thurston.

"Yes sir, we was right over it," Seaver said. "But he wouldn't give the command."

"Well, if he had, you'd probably all be lying out there now."

"Maybe so, sir."

"Sorry about your brother, Montrill," said

the major. "A fine boy and a good soldier."

"Thank you, sir," Montrill said humbly.

When Dr. Halversen returned from his examination of Dirk Herrold's body, he wore a perplexed expression. "That Indian must have got very close, Major. And it looks like he was using a Remington fifty."

Thurston nodded gravely. "An Apache can get on top of you before you know it, Hal. And naturally they have picked up all kinds of weapons."

"Of course," Halversen said. "I was only remarking, Tom."

There was a court of inquiry, merely a matter of form, and nothing new came of it. . . . But the rumor persisted that Derrick Herrold had been shot by one of his own troopers, for refusing to order his detail to the assistance of another column attacked by Geronimo and Hatchese with a hundred braves. The story reached Crispin at school, and he saw no reason to doubt it.

That had been five years ago, and now the third Herrold was at Burnside, this one by his own request. The cycle was complete, with Cris Herrold as reckless and rash as ever his father Justin had been. Hellfire Herrold all over again, the old-timers declared.

Men said that human lives meant nothing

to Crispin Herrold; he regarded all soldiers as expendable. Having had his father and mother die broken-hearted, his brother killed by a bullet in the back, it was true that death had lost some of its significance for Herrold. He was little concerned with the rest of humanity, and whether or not people lived or died.

Sooner or later death overtook everyone. The three who mattered to Cris Herrold had gone under before their time, and for those who went after them he had no grief to spare. Tragedy had made Herrold a fatalist. It was basically as simple as that.

Now, pacing the office floor, Herrold wondered how long it would be before this monotonous routine drove him mad. The paper work that he detested was palling on him, and he was corroded with shame at being set down in front of the whole post. Barron had served three or four months as adjutant. The Old Man would keep Herrold on the job at least that long, possibly longer. . . . It was too much to endure. He'd have to get a transfer or resign.

But he couldn't do either without defeating his own purpose. He had suffered out four years at the Point, after the disgrace of his dad and brother. Herrold should be able to take a few months of this. In the cruel lonely ordeal of his Cadet days, he had resolved to stick it out, seek an assignment to Burnside, and blaze a record that would wipe every last blot from the Herrold name. Thus far he had not succeeded, but he could not quit on the losing end. . . . No matter how much he revolted at office routine, Herrold had to hang on and wait for another chance.

One more thing held him here. His brother's murderer, or the clue to his identity, was still at Burnside, and he intended to bring that man to justice. It was characteristic of Cris Herrold not to think of Anita Raven or Tess Thurston in this respect. Girls had always come easy to him. Herrold didn't have to worry about them.

CHAPTER VI

There was little variation in the pattern of Herrold's days, as preparations went on for the special patrol Montrill and Ashley were to lead into the mountains. Shaddock's burial detail returned from Cathedral Rocks with haunted eyes and faces that were sickly pallid under the whiskers and tan and trail dirt. The sutler's whiskey sales went up that evening. Montrill and Ashley, assisted by Dunleavy and Seaver, were personally inspecting horses, saddle gear and equipment for their mission. Lieutenant Barron took a detachment south into the Cherokee Valley. . . . And Herrold sat at his desk, brooding over forms and reports and general orders in triplicate, or handing them half-read to the orderly, a studious clerical corporal who would have made an ideal post adjutant.

Reveille and roll call in morning grayness, fatigue and stables, mess and drill and recall. Herrold watched it all from the office windows fronting the long sunbaked rectangle. The slow heat-laden drag of afternoon, platoons sweating at close-order drill, the shadows lengthening at last. Retreat, with the flag lowered in the waning light, and night climbing the slopes, welling into the sky, spreading over the earth, still and dark and smothering. Sentry calls relayed from gate to gate on the hour, tattoo trilling through light-and-shadow on the parade, and finally the slow sorrowful lament of taps. . . . An existence measured and marked off by bugle calls, thought Herrold, as barren and sterile as the blare of brass itself.

Back from the Cherokee with a fresh grouch and a fiery sunburn, Ray Barron stomped into the adjutant's office, advertising his surly resentment. Herrold looked up without pleasure or welcome, not liking this man and his assumption that they were kindred spirits because they had attended West Point. Something about Barron made Herrold ashamed of certain stupid speeches he had been guilty of in Anita Raven's hearing, on the subject of officers and gentlemen.

"Not an Indian in a hundred miles south," Barron said. "That's why *I* was sent, of course. To exercise the horses and men!"

"And spread good will, Ray," amended Herrold.

Barron snorted. "Good will! The settlers are becoming as hostile as the Apaches. Ran into Kirby Tisdale and some of his Flying F cowhands, hunting for strayed cattle. They were so insolent, Tisdale in particular, that I was tempted to open fire on them. The other whites we saw acted the same way."

"They say Kirby Tisdale's quite a gun-fighter," mused Herrold.

"He's probably shot a few Mexicans and Indians. Imagine a character like him being tolerated as a guest in the commanding officer's house? Why, Tisdale ought to be horsewhipped off the post!"

"So Kirby's seeing Teresa again? She no doubt considers him a picturesque and romantic figure."

"Have you dropped her altogether, Cris?" asked Barron bluntly.

Herrold stiffened in his chair. "Is that any of your business, Ray?"

Barron flushed, visible even through the new sunburn. "Why, no, I just wondered about it. Certainly Tess is preferable to that half-breed Raven girl. I —"

"That's enough, Ray," said Herrold quietly. "You're getting out of line a bit — for a gentleman."

"I'm sorry, Cris." Barron gestured with angered embarrassment. "Has it occurred to you, Cris, that there is a great deal of discrimination here?"

The fellow was voicing Herrold's own thoughts, but Cris pretended to be puzzled. "On the part of whom?"

"You know as well as I do! The Old Man, of course. He can see nobody but Montrill and Ashley. And you'd think Raven was the C.O. here."

"Well, they are proven men."

Barron grunted in disgust. "All right, if you're satisfied, why should I complain? But it looks as if neither of us will get out in the field again. Not where it counts anyway. You'd think Thurston would show some consideration to Academy men."

"He's been out here a long time," Herrold said. "And before that he fought through the war. West Point is a long way behind him. Perhaps Thurston feels that officers from the Point are better qualified for paper work than for field duty."

Barron shook his glossy head and touched his prominent peeling nose. He had come here expecting sympathy, union in a common grievance against authority, and he was being rejected at every turn. This Herrold was flighty, unpredictable, slightly unbalanced perhaps. . . . Barron sighed wearily. "Well, this is an unorthodox and haphazard type of combat."

"You can't fight Indians from a text book," Herrold conceded. "Nor from an office desk."

Barron reared up ponderously, lips tautened in a sneer, broad face mottled scarlet and purple. "To what do you owe your notable success then, Herrold?"

Herrold stood up quickly, tall, straight and slender before the other's solid bulk. "You'd better go, Barron. And I won't require any more assistance from you. I believe I have mastered the intricate problems of this position."

"Well, by God!" gasped Barron, glaring with hooded bloodshot eyes. "I thought you might want *one* friend at Burnside!"

Herrold's refined features were calm, cold, and mildly scornful. "If I do, I'll select the one," he said, clipped and precise. "Now I have work to do, Barron." He smiled mockingly and shuffled papers on the desk. "Work of vital importance and priority."

"You don't scare me, mister!" blustered Barron. "You're poison, as they say, but *I* don't scare. And I don't forget either!"

"I'm sure you don't," Herrold said. "Good afternoon, sir."

"You'll be sorry for this, mister! I was your last chance. Nobody else in this post'll come within twenty feet of a polecat like you. I stood the stink because of the Academy, but I'm all through now. You're strictly on your own, plebe, and all alone. You'll probably end up like your brother Dirk did, too."

Herrold stepped lithely around the desk. "Maybe you know more about that than you ever admitted, Barron?"

The larger man fell back involuntarily before the naked deadly menace in Crispin Herrold. "If I did, I wouldn't tell you, mister."

"Maybe I'll beat it out of you sometime," Herrold said tonelessly. "Or hack it out with a saber. Or shoot it out with a gun."

"You're crazy," panted Barron. "You're insane, mister. You ought to be locked up — and I think you will be!" He wheeled and tramped heavily from the room, hands knotted into huge reddened fists at his sides, massive shoulders hunched with pent-up fury.

Herrold watched him go without expression, thinking in idle wonder: What makes me do and say things like that? I'm enough of a lone wolf here, as he said, without seeking further isolation. That poor crud meant well, I suppose, but he goes against my grain, and I couldn't resist needling him. . . . Herrold laughed, silently and mirthlessly. Everybody and everything went against his grain for that matter. Why, he must be the cross-grained one himself, the misfit and outcast. . . . *Only Anita and Tess put up with me, and they won't forever.* Nita'll go to Montrill, Tess to Kirby Tisdale, and where will I be? . . . Well, I'll still have my own private mission. There really isn't room in my life for anything or anyone else.

After retreat, guard mount and supper that evening, Montrill's expedition made ready for departure in the night. Herrold and other officers drifted out of their adobes to watch from the row, while across the parade troopers gathered before the barracks. Awareness of the significance and danger of this mission filled the quadrangle with more than the usual tension. Herrold felt it. Teresa Thurston felt it at the head of officers' row, and Anita Raven walking in from her cabin. Everybody in Burnside was under the strain. Anita paused twenty paces from Herrold, apart from all of them. When he beckoned, Anita shook her shining dark head and remained where she was, staring across the parade.

Lanterns flashed and glimmered about the stables, and the troopers came out leading their horses and making last-minute adjustments. The general impression was of tall rangy men, lean, tough, and a little cocky, rawboned bronze faces sculptured in lamplight. They moved well, but their disregard for the regulation uniform displeased Herrold. Campaign hats to suit individual fancies, worn every which way, more like cowboys than cavalrymen. Scarfs and bandannas at their necks. Some holsters flapless and cut-down, in the fashion of Western gunmen. Jackets half-buttoned, boots and belts unpolished. . . . But they were fine fighting men, for all this laxity, Herrold acknowledged.

It was three days out and three back, with luck. They had rations for a week, a cantle-roll oat issue, three hundred rounds of carbine ammunition, and a hundred for hand-guns, per man. There was some joshing and laughter as they lined up, but less than customary. Vermilya called from the barrack wall, "Don't hurry back, Bucky. I'll take good care of that money." And Thackston replied, laughing: "You invest that in poker and whiskey, boy; I'll take it out of your hide!" Sergeant Seaver grumbled at them to get formed up and count off. In front of Thurston's quarters, big Montrill, little Ashley, and the buckskin-garbed Raven were talking to the Old Man and other staff officers.

Herrold's eyes flicked back to the line of men standing beside their horses. Montrill had chosen them well. Old Seaver and the jut-jawed Dunleavy for sergeants, with Corporals McCord and Shiller, and twenty-one troopers. Most of them wouldn't shine in dress parade, but they were the best available as far as action in the field went. More fighters than soldiers, which was what you needed in a war like this. Dallas, the Texas bronc buster; Crater, the badman from Kansas; Red Fennell, runaway black sheep of an old Massachusetts family; roughnecks like Ox Hendree and Ginter; devil-may-care kids like Thackston, Cantey and Lemonick; and Rocky Flint, ex-prizefighter and barroom bouncer in New York.

Rabble and riffraff, Herrold had termed them, and Anita Raven had promptly and justifiably called him for it. Hardly more than two would pass his inspection. Ullrich, with his German blood, had a proper respect for the uniform. Silk Slocum, the former Mississippi gambler, was a dandy by nature. The rest dressed for comfort and utility, but even so Herrold had lied in his teeth when he spoke so disparagingly of them. Hardened campaigners, great horsemen and deadly shots, they were the equal of any cavalrymen in the world. . . . All at once Herrold felt a rising quickening pride in them, and wished he were going out with them, one of them, really belonging the way Montrill and Ashley did.

"The detail's formed, sir," reported Sergeant Seaver.

Montrill and Ashley moved to their mounts, Raven holding back with his, and the line was straight and stiff now. "Prepare to mount. Mount!" There was the surge and thud of bodies hitting leather in unison, the snort of horses, creak of saddle gear, and the clink-clank of metal equipment. "Left by twos, march!" Bridles made a faint jingle through the murmur of leather, the clop of hoofbeats, and dust swirled up yellow in the lamps of the rectangle. The smell of saddle soap, oiled steel, sweated leather and flannel rode with the column, and every eye in the fort followed the riders toward the main gate.

Crispin Herrold's heart soared strangely in his chest, a lump of pain rose in his throat, and his spine tingled from base to neck. He hadn't felt that way since his plebe days, before the news of that massacre on the Querhada, and he marveled at it. . . . There went a compact fighting unit, with splendid spirit and morale, a living tribute to Montrill and Ashley. Two lieutenants, four non-commissioned officers, twenty-one men, and scout Jim Raven.

Herrold wondered how many of those twenty-eight would be coming back to Burnside. He thought he had observed Anita Raven's gray gaze on Montrill, even more than on her father. . . . But it was not that which made him confess envy of another man for the first time. It was the kind of a leader Montrill was, and the way the men followed him.

Then Herrold shrugged and laughed with returning cynicism at himself. That desk job must be softening him up, mentally as well as physically. . . . He turned to look for Anita Raven, but the girl was gone. Well, he had a date with her later anyway. Tonight with Jim away, they'd have complete privacy in the log house at the far corner. Perhaps I'll exert a little more pressure tonight, Herrold thought, and make sure she forgets all about Rick Montrill.

CHAPTER VII

Major Thurston looked up from the outdated *Harper's Weekly,* as Teresa emerged from her bedroom. She had changed into a blue dress with white collar and cuffs, and looked fresh, vivacious and lovely, her hair piled in a high shimmering crown of gold, her blue eyes dancing with a gay challenge. Thurston, his mind still with Montrill's detail, had not been deriving much from the printed pages. Laying the magazine aside, he regarded her with warm admiration, and then frowned sternly.

"You're deserting the army again tonight, Tess?"

"What makes you think so?"

"I saw Kirby Tisdale and Bowie Hulpritt ride in."

Teresa laughed merrily. "Oh, Dad, you see everything, know everything!"

"Not quite — or I wouldn't be going into my dotage in a sagebrush outpost." Thurston smiled to erase the bitterness of his words. "A shame to waste that shining beauty on a cowhand, Tess."

She tossed her head. "Kirby's the foreman, as you know. And he's a man, all man."

"Yes, I guess he is," the major said. "But we have some of them too, you know."

"The two I'm thinking of," sighed the girl, "are too indifferent. Either they're afraid of your rank, Major or they just don't like blondes." She laughed and rumpled his gray hair. "Now Kirby Tisdale's afraid of nothing, and appreciative of fairness in a woman."

"He would have made an excellent cavalry officer."

"Why, that's high praise, coming from you, Dad!"

"It is," Thurston said soberly. "I think Tisdale's a good man. A trifle rough and wild, like the country, but generally well tempered and controlled. These Westerners seem to respect womanhood, for the most part. But I wouldn't go too far with the flirting and teasing, Tess. They cannot be dangled on a string like cadets."

"Don't you worry Dad. I can take care of myself. And handle anything from plebes to generals — or ranch ramrods."

"Over-confidence is a thing to be avoided,

daughter. In the field, the ballroom, or lover's lane. Remember that, Teresa."

"Yes, sir. Thank you, sir!" She kissed his furrowed brow, snapped into attention, saluted with a bright smile, and went out the front door onto the lean-to veranda.

Thurston stared after her, missing her dead mother with all the old aching hunger and loneliness dazed with memories. . . . After a painful interval he thrust it aside, picked up the *Harper's* and resumed reading. But his thoughts kept reverting to that column on its north-westerly night march along the upper Cherokee into the massed mountain wilderness of the Osages.

Teresa rounded the corner outside, passing between her adobe and the one occupied by Captain Jepson and his wife, moving into the moonlit rear area toward the deep shadows of the stockade wall. Kirby Tisdale was lounging in the habitual place, shoulders on the upright logs, a cigarette in his pleasant smiling lips. He came to meet her with lazy slouching grace, not a particularly big man but obviously one to be reckoned with. It was in the rugged leanness of his features and limber body, whipped rawhide tough from an outdoor life in the saddle. Kirby Tisdale had the cool quiet assurance of a man who was tops in his trade, and considered himself the equal, at least of anybody alive.

His smile was friendly as a boy's, but something was troubling Kirby Tisdale this night. Teresa saw it in the smoky slateness of his triangular-squinted eyes, the sharp set of cheekbones and jaws. He wore a cord jacket, polka dot neckerchief, clean white shirt, trim checked California pants tucked into heavy-stitched boots, high-heeled and silver-spurred. A low-slung gun was strapped on his right leg. The hat he held in hand was flat of crown and wide of brim. To Teresa, accustomed to the severe sameness of uniforms, he was as colorful and exciting a figure as Herrold had intimated to Barron.

"What's wrong, Kirby?" asked the girl noting his silence and the flash of his narrowed eyes, the thrust of his tousled head.

"Lost a hundred head, Tess. Two riders killed and scalped. We asked your father for help before. We're entitled to it, practically next door to the fort. He wouldn't give us any, but he'll have to now."

"I'm sorry, Kirby. But you don't know the army. Dad can't do a lot of things he'd like to."

"Forrester's goin' to write to Washington."

"That won't do any good. Dad's acting

95

under their command. The army has to protect the whole area, not just one ranch."

Kirby Tisdale laughed. "Yeah, they're doin' quite a job of it. Another year and there won't be a spread left in the Cherokee."

"They're doing what they can, with what they've got!" Teresa said, touched with anger.

"It don't seem to be enough," Tisdale drawled. "Look, Tess. What good is this drillin' and loafin' around the fort? Some of these soldiers could just as well be ridin' for us."

"You won't find any loafing in this post, Kirby. The army can't assign troopers to ride herd for you. If they did it for the Flying F, they'd have to do it for all the ranches.

"But ours is the biggest layout, and the best."

"Then the smaller poorer ones need help more than you do."

Tisdale swung his hat impatiently. "No use arguin' with you, Tess."

"You'll find it easier than arguing with the major, Kirby."

"I know, I know," he muttered. "The army runs by the book; can't see an inch beyond regulations. Reckon that's why they do so many fool things out here."

"*Wait* a minute, cowboy!" warned Teresa Thurston. "You can't talk that way about the army to me, Kirby."

Tisdale laughed softly. "Now take it calm and easy gal. I'm a man that speaks his mind. About the army or anythin' else. . . . But I never meant to waste all this moonlight in debatin'."

Teresa looked at him coldly, clearly, as if seeing him for the first time, and not liking what she saw. "Don't speak too freely to me, on certain subjects. I was born in an army hospital and grew up with the Third Regiment."

"That don't make it perfect, Tess."

"If you and your tough gun-slinging buckaroos are so good, take care of your own range!" she flared. "Don't come crying to the cavalry that you pretend to detest so."

Tisdale grinned ruefully. "All right, Tess, I'm sorry. We would if we had enough hands, but we just haven't got 'em."

With Tisdale subdued, Teresa was immediately chastened. "I'm sorry too Kirby. About your riders and cattle — and everything. But my father doesn't have a free rein here. I wish you'd try to understand that."

"Sure, sure." Tisdale laughed and swept her into his strong arms. "You're a regular little spitfire hellcat, Tess. Spoiled some from chousin' around these pretty boys in brass buttons. But you're my gal." Crushing her in a steel grip, he bent and kissed her with rising hunger and increasing force.

Teresa Thurston was responding with arms and mouth when something struck a chill note of warning in her brain. Something her father had said, combined with the sudden iron ruthlessness of this forthright man's embrace. She started to squirm and struggle in an effort to free herself, but this time Kirby Tisdale did not release her. His hold tightened even more, the pressure of his mouth bruising her lips against her teeth.

Wrenching her head aside, Teresa panted: "Let me go!"

"I'm not takin' orders tonight," Tisdale said, clamping onto her writhing shoulders. "Not even from the major's daughter."

"Please — Kirby!" she cried, fighting furiously against him.

"All right, woman!" Abruptly he held her at arms' length, his fingers biting into the firm flesh of her shoulders. "What is this anyway? I'm not one of your toy soldiers. You can't play games with me!"

"What do you mean?" The words jerked from her sore lips, as he shook her violently.

"Mean? What did all the kissin' and lovin' mean? You can't lead a man on forever, Tess. Your tinhorn cadets maybe, but not a real man. The time comes when your hand's called, lady. Either you got the cards or you got to pay off!" Tisdale's face was slit-eyed, hollow-cheeked, and drawn to the bone.

"I still don't know," gasped Teresa, her golden head weaving in desperation.

Kirby Tisdale's laugh was harsh, jeering. "What do they teach you in them fancy Eastern schools ma'am? Well, I'm goin' to teach you what they didn't. A lesson you sure got comin' to you, gal." He drew her in close again, bending her back, groping for her mouth with his own, grinding her lissome rounded form against his sinewy hardness. Tess strained to break away but was completely overpowered, the breath forced from her lungs, the strength seeping from her body. She couldn't scream with Tisdale's lips fastened on hers. . . . It comes to this raw final brutality, she thought. This is what Dad tried to warn me about. What Montrill tried to tell me with his gray eyes.

And this was the scene Crispin Herrold came upon, when he stepped from the rear of his 'dobe to walk the lane behind officers' row toward the Raven cabin, a way he often took to forestall some of the wagging tongues within the camp. The interlocked couple swayed from shadow to moonbeams, and Herrold hesitated until he was positive the girl was trying to fight off the man. Then he strode forward and caught Tisdale's shoulder yanking the Westerner loose, spinning him around and away from Teresa Thurston.

Kirby Tisdale came about with the big .44 Colt leaping into his right hand, and Herrold saw what they meant about the quickness of these Arizona gunmen. He had left off his belt and holster, and he spread his hands to signify that he was unarmed.

"Men get killed for less than that," Tisdale said. "I've killed 'em for far less, soldier."

"You want me to get a gun?" inquired Herrold.

"And bring the guard back with you?" Tisdale laughed. "Why don't you mind your own business, soldier?"

"Miss Thurston was trying to get away from you, Tisdale. That made it my business. Tess, you'd better go in."

But the girl only withdrew into the stockade shadow, and Herrold could see her blonde head and shoulders trembling as she leaned on the wall, face hidden in her hands.

"You take advantage of that uniform," Tisdale said, the Colt hanging loosely in his hand. "You know I can't lift a gun against the uniform."

"Get back to your ranch then," advised Herrold.

Kirby Tisdale surged forward, snarling, the gun barrel lifted: "Why, you damn tinhorn dude!"

Herrold stood his ground, straight and firm, slim and elegant in front of the crouching gunman. Tisdale halted uncertainly, cursing and shoving the Colt back into its sheath, fingering the large silver buckle. "I can drop this belt. We can have it barehanded."

"Drop it," Herrold said, reaching for the buttons of his immaculate uniform coat.

"No, *no!*" Teresa Thurston pushed herself from the vertical logs. "I won't allow it. You'd better leave, Kirby."

"You asked me here, Tess," reminded Tisdale.

"Yes, I did. And now I'm asking you to go, Kirby." Her voice sounded shaky and tired.

Kirby Tisdale's teeth grated audibly, his face convulsing darkly. "All right, Tess, play with your two-bit soldiers, but leave the men alone." He turned to Herrold. "All I want is to meet you somewhere outside of here."

Herrold nodded. "When you do, don't let the uniform stop you."

"Nothin'll stop me," Tisdale said. "Nothin'll keep you from dyin', soldier."

"The lady asked you to leave," Herrold said flatly.

"I'm goin'. But I'll be seein' you, boy. And when I do you want to fill your hand — or try to." With a mocking flip of his hand, Kirby Tisdale stalked away with the stilted grace of a man who had spent most of his life astride a horse.

Herrold watched him out of sight, and moved to Teresa's side. "Barron was right about one thing, at least. That fellow should be horsewhipped off the grounds."

"No, Cris. It was my fault, I'm afraid. I've been an awful fool." She laughed, a shallow nervous sound. "I hope he won't cause you any trouble, Crispin. He's killed men in gunfights."

"Don't worry about that, Teresa," said Herrold, smiling. "To get me, he'd have to come to the adjutant's office in headquarters. Are you all right, Tess?"

"Yes, and I want to thank you, Cris." She stood close to him, one hand on his sleeve, her fragrance rising to his nostrils, swirling pleasantly in his senses.

"It was nothing, Tess." Herrold studied

the soft lovely contours of her face in the moonlight, the clear breathtaking line of her throat and chin, and felt his blood quicken with excitement. He hadn't realized the desirability of this girl. It had taken a cowboy to make him fully conscious of her. Herrold smiled to himself, almost forgetting that he had been on his way to see Anita Raven.

"What did you see in him, Teresa?" he asked, taking her arm and turning back toward the Thurston quarters at the head of the row.

"I don't know exactly. He's attractive — and different. And I was bored and lonely, I guess."

Herrold smiled, with all his charm. "Tired of army officers, Tess?"

"No-o. But the ones that interested me were too aloof, Cris." She glanced up at him with fluttering eyelashes, pressing her shoulder against his chest.

He had thought she was a silly, flirtatious child, but Teresa Thurston was all woman, full-blown, mature and sensuous, and Herrold was abruptly and deliciously aware of it. He wondered what had kept him away from Tess, turned him to Anita Raven. Some deep-seated sense of inferiority perhaps, that made him feel unworthy of the major's daughter and sent him to a half-breed girl in a log cabin? . . . Why, he and Teresa were of similar backgrounds, the old line military aristocracy. They fitted and belonged together.

"The ones?" he pursued, knowing that she referred to Montrill and himself, feeling an unreasonably pang of jealousy. Always that damnable Confederate Montrill.

"The one, I really meant to say," Teresa murmured. "But I didn't quite dare to, Cris." It was much nicer, she decided, to be with a gentleman of her own class. Especially one as handsome, polished and debonair as Crispin Herrold. His remote indifference had driven her into Kirby Tisdale's arms in the first place. His and Montrill's.

"That's better, Tess," said Herrold, shortening and slowing his stride to match hers, stirred by her nearness.

Then, without quite knowing how it happened, they had stopped walking and were facing one another in the shadowy dimness, drawn strongly together and merging into one, their arms laced tight as their lips met and fused with sweet racing fire, held lingeringly. . . . They had kissed before but never like this. Parting at last, awed and breathless, they stared wonderingly into each other's eyes.

"Tess, we've wasted a lot of time," Herrold said slowly.

"Yes, Crispin," whispered Teresa, brilliant eyes intent and worshipful on his fine face. "But we have lots of time left, too."

There was one witness to this scene in the moon-dappled darkness behind officers' row. Anita Raven had been walking in to meet Cris Herrold. She halted at the sight of them, stood stricken for a moment, turned and ran swiftly back toward the cabin at the far end of the enclosure. Her eyes were dry and no sound came from her, except for her hard breathing, but there was a terrible tearing deep inside her breast. It went on and on, long after she had flung herself on the bed, and it seemed as if it never would cease.

Chapter VIII

The column had left the upper reaches of the Cherokee, traversed the rock and sage foothills, past Redstone Butte and The Spires, to strike through the main Osage Range, the towering triple peaks of Three Chiefs a constant landmark on the northern horizon. Jim Raven rode with the point, Montrill and Ashley alternating between there and the main body. Dunleavy and Seaver were out with flankers, and McCord and Shiller took turns at bringing up the rear guard. There were Indians before and around them, but keeping a distance and not even resorting to long-range sniping. Their presence was felt nevertheless, an incessant pressure that wore nerves raw and thin in the ranks.

The detail climbed Chickasaw Pass to the divide, and descended Cadnac Cut on the northern slopes. Below there was a break in the mountains, an upland desert and stone monument country, patterned crazily with ravines, potholes and tortuous canyons, twisting among gaunt buttes, angular mesas and razorbacked ridges. A nightmare terrain marked by the high-spreading candelabra of sahuaro cactus and clusters of many-bladed ocotillo and yucca, tangled with creosote and buckbrush and all varieties of desert growth. Here the Apaches harvested their mesquite beans and the mescal they baked, two staples of the Indian diet.

On the third day they crossed this arid expanse, known as Hellsgate Heights, plodding through the murderous heat and endless dust. As the afternoon burned away, Castle Rock loomed in monstrous grandeur ahead of them, and beyond it the twin pinnacles of The Brothers, with more mountains shouldering skyward on either side. The pace had been hard, and even the toughest troopers were saddle-galled and weary to the bone, sun-blinded and alkali-choked, their energy blighted and sapped by this savage climate and country.

The Apaches had faded, as they invariably did at this point, but alertness was even more essential in the column. Always before, the enemy had vanished entirely here, but this time they might be fanning out to flank and strike at the cavalry before sundown.

There was the usual grumbling and grousing along the line, but none of the venomous spite that infected the ranks when they followed Cris Herrold.

"Ain't no percentage in bein' a good soldier," growled Pop Ginter, the sour balding veteran. "The best men always get the worst jobs."

"That's the highest honor in the service, Pop," said Ullrich, the blond Prussian.

Ginter told him explicitly what to do with the honor, and the service too.

At the point, Montrill and Raven were scanning the great spired butte of Castle Rock, lofty and crimsoned in the lowering sun, flanked by sheer shale-drifted cliffs. Higher in the background rose The Brothers, and somewhere in the rugged highlands between the massive butte and those twin cones might be the lodges of Hatchese's central camp.

"No place up there for cavalry, Jim," said Montrill.

"Hatchese probably figured likewise. No, Monty, we'll have to pull them down outa there some way. Never get in there with any big force."

"You think this is the place, then?"

Jim Raven nodded. "Always thought so, Monty. But until we got them Winchesters I didn't think we was ready for the whole pack."

"I guess we weren't," Montrill said. "How many has he got, Jim?"

"Maybe five hundred fightin' bucks, I'd say offhand."

Montrill smiled wryly. "And we could put perhaps two hundred in the field, if we scrape the barrel."

"That's enough, Monty," said Jim Raven. "If we can get 'em out in the open at all, where we can hit 'em solid. That's enough, with them new repeaters, Monty."

Montrill was eyeing the rock walls again. "Any way up those cliffs, Jim?"

"That east one can be clumb — by a small party." Raven pointed a long bony finger. "Horses as far as that ledge there. On foot the rest of the way. Not easy, but it can be done."

"Maybe we'll do some climbing tonight," Montrill said thoughtfully.

The sun went down in flames beyond the western ramparts of the Osages, and the lurid colors softened and drained from the horizon. Heat lingered on the barren earth, the sky held its pale light, but there was relief from overhead glare and the sun's stunning impact. Men and horses breathed easier in the lavender twilight. There would be no fighting now, for the Apache religion was against night warfare. Jim Raven found a trickle of water in a sheltered ravine, and the column filed in there to bivouac.

Montrill was thinking hard as he posted sentries and unsaddled his bay gelding in the quick-gathering darkness. All around him men were unsaddling, watering and rubbing down their sweat-rimed mounts, examining hoofs and legs, stretching their own cramped limbs and washing up in the tiny creek. The horses picketed, small cook-fires began to glow under the paloverde trees, and soon the odor of frying bacon and boiling coffee sharpened the air. It had been too hot to eat much at noon. Now, refreshed by water, tobacco smoke and evening coolness, the troopers were ravenously hungry.

None of the plans they had discussed seemed very satisfactory. Montrill had permission to act on his own initiative, and he meant to make some attempt to draw out the Apaches in full force. The best method he could devise was to climb that cliff with a small party and rouse the enemy, while the main column went back to Burnside after K and L troops. The small group would have to play hide-and-seek with the Indians until Major Thurston arrived in strength. It wasn't much of a scheme, but it might break this long stalemate.

Hatchese wouldn't leave his mountain stronghold to face a large force of cavalry, but he'd come down and scour the country after a detail. The decoy group would have little chance of survival, but with Jim Raven along they'd have some chance. It was better than risking a major part of the detachment. The diversion unit would be more mobile than a bigger crew. The Burnside-bound column must be strong enough to fight its way home, if necessary. . . . It was simple elementary strategy, but it seemed about the best they could manage. Only Jim Raven's presence made it at all plausible.

Montrill ate mechanically with the rest, wolfing the bacon, sopping the grease with hardtack, washing it down with black coffee. Afterward they rolled cigarettes, filled pipes, or bit off chews, and settled back to relax and rest, sidearms and carbines close at hand.

The matter of personnel offered complications. Montrill had tentatively decided on a party of five to go up the cliff, three others with Jim Raven and himself. He intended to have Ashley lead the detail back to the post, but Ash insisted on staying as one of the scouts. There was never any question of rank between them. Ashley wore the shoulder bar of a first lieutenant, but Montrill had been given this command. . . . Montrill sighed and motioned Ashley now, and Ash moved around the ruby embers and sat down beside him, backs against a boulder.

"I wish you'd stay with the detail, Ash."

"Seaver or Dunleavy can take it back as well as anyone, Rick," said Ashley. "I want to ride this one out with you."

"I was going to take Seav and Dunny."

"One of them, Rick. And one of the corporals."

"All right, Ash. We'll let them draw for it." Montrill broke off some brittle forage grass at the base of the rock, and called the four noncoms, explaining the situation. All four of them promptly volunteered for the cliff climbing, but Montrill made them each select a grass blade from his closed hand. "The longs to Burnside. The shorts with me."

Sergeant Seaver and Corporal Shiller pulled the longer stalks and swore disgustedly, while Dunleavy and McCord solemnly congratulated one another.

"We ain't paid to command a whole column, Monty," muttered Seaver, his seamed face scowling and sullen.

"Maybe you'll get a commission out of it,

Seav," prodded Dunleavy, winking and grinning at the others.

Seaver cursed and mentioned a rather unusual repository for that and all commissions. "That's an order, Lieutenant?" he asked, and succumbed into stony silence as Montrill nodded. Shiller said, "We'll live longer anyway, Seav," but Seaver refused to be cheered.

Jim Raven joined them for a council of war, after which Montrill gave Seaver and Shiller their final instructions, and set to drafting a written message and a map of their position for Major Thurston. "Get to Burnside as soon as possible, and have the major march at once. We'll have these hills swarming with Indians for him to round up. Prepare to start about three hours from now, resting in the meantime. . . . Good luck, Seav." Montrill held out his hand, and Seaver grasped it with a slow smile.

"You're the ones goin' to need luck, Monty. The best of it to you anyway."

There was a general round of handshaking, and then Montrill's detachment started getting ready to move with the rising of the moon.

"How'd they let us get so close?" Ashley asked, buckling on his gun belt.

"Hatchese may leather somebody for

that," Jim Raven said. "But more likely they're countin' on butcherin' us for breakfast in the mornin'."

"Getting over-confident," Ashley remarked.

"Can't blame them much for that, Ash," said Montrill dryly.

"No, they've been running the show so far," Ashley admitted.

Raven chuckled. "With a little luck, we're goin' to change that, boys."

Chapter IX

The five men saddled up and left the defile without any fanfare, the sprawling troopers saluting and waving as they watched the departure. There was little comment, but every man in camp was thinking that they might never see those five again. The loss to Burnside would be inestimable. The two best officers in Montrill and Ashley, a scout of Raven's incomparable quality, and non-coms like Dunleavy and McCord. There was no measuring the personal loss either. Those five riders were well loved and highly respected in the cantonment.

The ground, a broken crazy patchwork of light and shadow under the moon, rose gradually as they moved north toward Castle Rock. The moon looked larger and brighter, the stars sparkled closer at this altitude. Spanish bayonet bloomed ghostly white, and ironwood trees raised spiny-branched boughs against the luminous night-blue heavens. As the hills lifted and rolled around them, there were scattered stands of ash, box elder, black cottonwood, and post oak. Higher slopes were dark with ponderosa pine and locust, or palely shimmering with aspen and birch.

Lank Jim Raven led the way with as much confidence as if he were crossing the parade at Burnside. It was reassuring and comforting just to glance at that long angular buckskin form, Montrill found. He regarded the others with equal approval. The slight, sharp-profiled Ashley, big rawboned Dunleavy with his craggy thrusting jaws, and the broad solid McCord. A man couldn't ask for better company to face danger and death with.

No matter how many times a man went out to meet death, he never quite grew resigned to the thought of dying, Montrill reflected, although he dreaded it somewhat less, as his years increased. Montrill's fear was rather of being badly wounded, or captured and tortured. Death wasn't so bad, if it came clean and quick. . . . Life became lonely and empty, as a man aged and those closest to him died. His parents had died while he was away fighting a senseless losing war. His friends had died in that war, his brother Lance down on the Aravaipa, and all the other comrades out here. Montrill had died a little with each one of them, and especially with Lance. That scene of slaughter and horror was branded forever in Montrill's mind, and there were still nights when he woke screaming soundlessly in a cold sweat from dreaming of it.

We could have saved Lance and most of the rest of them, Montrill thought with a bitterness that never lessened. If we'd driven down into them, the Apaches would have broken and run, never knowing that we were only thirty. At least there's a chance they would have. But that ornery West Point cadet of a Derrick Herrold wouldn't give the command. I know he was trying to live down his father's rashness, but that doesn't excuse it. I wonder who shot him. People who weren't there think Seaver or I did. Somebody'll shoot Cris Herrold the same way before he's through. I'd like to myself, but not that way. I'd want a fair stand-up fight of it. And we'll get to it some day — if we both live.

With a resolute effort Montrill brought himself back to the present and questioned the Indian scout about the east cliff, which looked as insurmountable as any part of the vast towering landmark.

"The Injuns know the trail," Jim Raven

said. "But they won't be watchin' it. They don't figure any whites know of it, or would be crazy enough to climb it if they did know."

Ashley grinned. "They have no idea how crazy us white men can get."

"What do you expect to find on top, Jim?" asked Montrill.

"Maybe a warrior camp, maybe nothin'. But I got a notion there'll be some kinda outpost anyway. You can see the whole Hellsgate from that rim. I was up there with an old mountain man, name of Pete Magner. He was real friendly with the Apaches. Could go 'most anywhere without 'em botherin' him. Saved my hair more times'n I could count, old Pete did."

They jogged onward in the eerie brilliance of moonlight and starshine, breaking the stillness with the chop of hoofs, the rustling creak of leather, jingling bridles and clinking metal, the grunt of horses and the breathing of men. Alkali dust spiraled up, and shod hoofs struck occasional sparks off the stones. A coyote howled sorrowfully and was answered from afar. An owl hooted and then another. When Raven halted the column, they could hear the faint stir and scrape of small earth creatures. The air smelled of blistered sand and rock, greasewood, sage, and once in a while the pure breath of pines.

Castle Rock reared directly overhead now, a thousand feet or so of almost vertical wall, and if Montrill hadn't known Jim Raven he would have doubted that man could ever scale those heights. They passed the central butte itself, and the eastern abutment did look a bit more accessible, although forbidding enough. "It's been quite a spell," the scout said, his falcon eyes sweeping the enormous barrier, settling at last on the spot they were seeking. Jim Raven always knew where he was going and what he was doing. They started the climb on broad switchback ledges, that gradually steepened and narrowed as they mounted the sheer face of the cliff.

"Pete Magner took me up here," Jim Raven said, when they paused to rest the horses. "Old Pete would of been worth a regiment to the army. Except he really liked Injuns. Better'n most whites, I reckon."

The natural ramp ended about halfway up the barrier on a substantial level shelf. They reached this three hours after leaving the ravine, at approximately the time Seaver should be starting his detail on the return trip. Leaving Dunleavy and McCord with the horses, Jim Raven and the two officers began the nearly perpendicular climb on foot, working their way up a rock chimney. Raven had his carbine slung, but Montrill and Ashley carried only their revolvers.

Emerging from the Chimney, they mounted along an open cliff. It was slow painful work, with Jim Raven picking his way carefully and meticulously, locating and testing hand- and foot-holds for the others to follow. Moonlight flooding the heights made the ascent possible. Sweating freely in the night, they toiled patiently upward, gripping with hand and toes, pressing their faces and bodies to the stone surface against the pressure that threatened to throw them out and down the mountainside. Montrill had little liking for this unaccustomed business. The beat of his heart seemed sufficient to dislodge him at any instant. Nervous strain combined with intense physical effort brought on nausea and dizziness.

Clambering to the clifftop at last, they lay panting on a talus slope that tapered in to the summit, weak and sick with relief, resting until their pulses slowed and their lungs ceased pumping so furiously and the sweat cooled and dried on their skin. "There's an easier way down, boys," Jim Raven reported cheerfully. Montrill rinsed his mouth with canteen water and murmured, "Thank God for that."

Refreshed and eased, they slogged upward in shale and gravel to the ultimate crest and relaxed once more against the rimrock. The land dropped away from the rim, and perhaps a hundred yards in front of them was a small camp of a dozen wickiups. A few braves sat about the campfire, but most of them were apparently sleeping. Beyond the lodges a score or so of ponies were picketed. Several dogs skulked and yapped around the reddish fringes of firelight. For some reason Montrill felt disappointed, as if he had expected to find the whole Apache nation here in one great village.

Raven swore then, Ashley exhaled audibly, and Montrill saw what they had seen a second sooner. Outside the ruddy glare of the fire, a white man was strung up, spread-eagled between two posts, naked except for tattered remnants of clothing, shaggy gray head drooping. The white flesh was striped and smeared darkly, and Montrill realized it was slashed with cuts and burns. As they watched, the prisoner raised his gray-bearded face slowly and screamed in the unbearable agony of returning consciousness.

"God Almighty, it looks like Pete Magner!" said Jim Raven, squinting his gray eyes and unslinging his Winchester. Montrill handed him the field glasses. Raven's hawk-face twisted as he focussed them on the victim. "Old Pete, as sure as shootin'. Now what could of turned them red devils on Pete Magner?"

An Indian rose from the fireside with a long lighted splinter of wood in his hand. Prancing over to the trussed-up white man, he gibbered and gesticulated in an idiotic manner, and then thrust the blazing splinter into Pete Magner's side, watching the flame eat toward the squirming flesh. Montrill writhed and cursed in helpless fury. Jim Raven returned the glasses and levered a shell into the chamber of his rifle. . . . Pete Magner, arms roped wide and high enough to dislocate his shoulders, shrieked and flogged about in frenzied anguish.

"No, by God!" said Jim Raven. "Pete's stood enough."

Ashley and Montrill exchanged glances. They hadn't planned to expose themselves and get the Apaches aroused this early in the game. It would shorten their chances of survival considerably. But this was too much to sit back and take, and that old prospector was a friend of Jim's. . . . Raven looked questioningly at them. Montrill nodded and drew his colt. "Go ahead, Jim." Ashley lifted his gun from the leather, his thin face mildly pleased at the decision.

"I owe Pete this much," Jim Raven said, lining and sighting his carbine.

The Winchester blasted and Raven's aim was true, the .44 striking and stilling forever the tortured figure of old Pete Magner. Levering quickly, Jim let go again, and the Apache who had planted the splinter jerked, spun and toppled at Magner's feet. The other Indians were scattering, bolting in panic, as Montrill and Ashley turned their pistols loose. It was long range for hand-guns, but Jim Raven was still working his Winchester. Another buck tripped and tumbled, headlong and howling, into the fire. The rest had fled out of view.

They emptied their weapons to keep the warriors pinned down in the vicinity of camp, reloaded, and dropped back down the talus slope. Jim Raven led them along the edge of the moon-whitened precipice to where a broad drift of shale and gravel poured down a break in the sheer rock wall. "We'll ride that down, boys," Raven said, waving them on and waiting on the rim with his carbine ready, in case the Indians rushed the topside.

It didn't look too inviting, but anything was better than that slow climb down.

Montrill took off in a long flying leap, sinking knee-deep in the dirt and starting a small landslide. Plunging and wallowing, driving hard with his legs, clawing and balancing with hands and arms, Montrill rode the roaring avalanche down toward the wide shelf where Dunleavy and McCord waited with the horses. The heavy rushing surge about Montrill's legs increased and deepened, finally spilling him into a hurtling roll. He wound up at last, thrashing to a stop in the gravel delta that spread along the ledge, breathless, bruised and shaken, choked and plastered with dirt.

Shots rang out overhead, muzzle flashes streaking palely in the moonbeams, and Montrill stood by to see that the others didn't override the shelf. Ashley came tobogganing down the steep chute, dust boiling up silvery against the stars, tossed like a chip in a torrent. Montrill caught him as he skidded wildly to the bottom and lay panting and gasping against Montrill's boots. They were laughing together when Jim Raven catapulted down out of the night in a storm of flying dirt, long arms and legs windmilling as he cartwheeled into the last stretch and slid to a groaning halt.

"What the devil's funny?" he panted, crawling upright. "All right for kids maybe.

No good for an old man. I feel all broke to pieces."

Beating gravel from their uniforms, they moved along the shelf to join the horse-holders, swing into the saddle, and start down the switchback ramp formed by projecting ledges. There wasn't likely to be any immediate pursuit tonight, but by morning Apaches would be all over the landscape. Montrill hoped they wouldn't discover at once that the main column had headed back for Burnside. His tiny command had two objectives now: to stay alive, and to keep the Indians too busy here to pursue Seaver's detail.

They reached the base of the cliff without mishap, and paused there under the bulwark of Castle Rock to check their guns and unplug barrels, empty dirt from their boots and shake it from their clothing, and to drink from their canteens. Jim Raven was studying where to spend the remainder of the night.

"We're really in the middle of it now, Montrill thought with a solemn smile. For at least six days and probably longer, we've got to play tag with these Apaches. Five men against five hundred. Running, hiding, fighting, waiting. And never knowing whether or not Seaver got through to Burnside.

Whether relief would come in a week, or a month — or not at all.

Well, Seaver would get the column back to the fort if anyone could. And with Jim Raven along, Montrill's little group had a thin outside chance of lasting and living.

"I always told old Pete they'd turn on him," Raven said, more to himself than anyone else. "He never would believe it of 'em. But they sure turned all right. Must of worked on him wicked, to make Pete Magner yell like that."

CHAPTER X

Sergeant Seaver had turned them out of bivouac and got them moving back across Hellsgate Heights three hours after Montrill's detachment left. It wasn't a pleasant chore. The brief rest had stiffened men and beasts alike, and they were sullen and irritable as they filed southward. The mountain night was cold enough to stiffen sweated saddle leather and uniforms, ache in lame joints and set the troopers to shivering and swearing. Seaver thought it would have been better if they'd turned back right after mess instead of taking that break.

They hadn't progressed far when the distant gunfire broke out on the heights behind them, echoing and reverberating down the cliffs of Castle Rock. Seaver halted the column, thinking morbidly: That's bad. They've jumped them already. Now what could've gone wrong back there? Jim's too smart to walk into a trap. Indians aren't supposed to attack at night, and our boys aren't dumb enough to open up on them this early. Something must have broke bad, and that just about cooks them five. I hope none of them get taken prisoner.

"We turnin' back, Seav?" asked Corporal Shiller, slim and graceful in his saddle at the sergeant's side.

"You know our orders, Shill," said Seaver gruffly, his scarred face bleak and tobacco-lumped under the campaign hat. He raised his voice. "Move along, men! Close up the intervals there; close up." The tired horses lunged forward again, the riders grumbling and cursing, their ears cocked back to that faint crackling of gunshots in the rear.

Moonlight washed the choppy wastelands with an unreal brightness, jeweling the mica particles in earth and rock. Grotesque stone pillars threw even weirder shadows across the sand dunes. Golden gilia glittered like tinsel, and barrel cactus loomed dispropor-tionately large in the tricky light. The air streamed and sparkled, and shade-patterns seemed to shift unnaturally on the ground. There was beauty in the desert night, but Seaver did not care for it.

Seaver didn't like any part of this. Chew-ing the tobacco that had gone dry in his mouth, he cursed Monty and Ash for leaving him in command here. Why, if he'd ever wanted the responsibility he'd have made officer years ago. Lieutenant anyway, probably captain by now. But he didn't want the authority any more than the responsibility. And here he was with twenty-two lives on his hands, and Burnside hell-and-gone over the hump of the Osages. It beat the dickens what a man got wished onto him in this mucked-up world.

And we'll have Apaches on our necks by morning, Seaver thought. They'll spot where we split up and headed back, and they'll come hellity-hooping down on us at two or three to one, maybe worse. We'll have them all the way back, hounding our tail, chewing at our flanks, and we can't stop to fight; we've got to keep moving. I ought to send a rider on ahead before they hit us, but I hate to send a man alone across this country. I won't until I have to do it. . . . If we can make Cadnac Cut maybe, if we can get over the mountains, we'll have a chance.

The burden of command bothered Seaver, nagged and wore on him. Some of the best friends he had left were in this column. Tex Dallas, Rocky Flint, Charley Crater, Pop Ginter. . . . Young Cantey and Lemonick, Lafferty and Bucky Thackston, Red Fennell and Slate Dillon. They were all good men:

Ullrich, Stonesifer, little Tut Jarnigan, big Ox Hendree, and the rest. And back there on Castle Rock were five he counted among the finest he had ever known. Five who might be dead or dying this minute.

Long after midnight and perhaps halfway across the shimmering wastes of Hellsgate, Seaver stopped the exhausted detail and bivouacked again. They had to have more rest, in order to endure tomorrow's merciless heat. He hated to get caught this side of the Osages, but the horses and men had reached their limit. Seaver hoped to make the foot of Cadnac Cut before the Apaches caught up with them. He knew with sickening surety that they'd be coming. . . .

Seaver's premonition was correct. They were gulping coffee in the wan lemon-colored light of morning before sunup, when enemy crossfire ripped at them from the rear flanks. There was no time to get the column in motion, but cover was adequate and the picket-line was well sheltered in a deep arroyo. Still chewing coffee-soaked hardtack and voicing profane disgust at having their breakfast interrupted, the troopers ducked under cover and unleashed their carbines from boulders, malpais rims, squat greasewood shrubs, and catclaw-shrouded potholes.

Only young Gussy Karras was firing blindly, and Seaver said kindly: "Steady, Gus, boy. Wait for a target and make 'em count." The kid turned with a white-lipped grimace of a grin, and stopped wasting ammunition at once. His first time out, Seaver recollected, and wondered why Karras had been chosen. . . . Gray morning vapors wreathed the rock columns and faulted terrain. The Indians were flitting shadows on the misted flanks, lighted by muzzle-blasts. If they'd been smart, they would have surrounded the detail, cut it off from the mountain passes ahead. But they couldn't wait, Seaver thought.

His veterans were holding their fire, searching for marks in the shifting fog, and Seaver smiled with quiet pride, huddled behind the basalt outcrop. In action they didn't require any orders. There was Cantey, crooning to himself as he cradled the Winchester and peered through white-blossomed bayonet bush. Charley Crater, the Kansas killer, wishing they'd come within six-gun range. Tex Dallas, firing intermittently and drawling curses in a lazy almost-friendly fashion. Fennell, the fugitive from Harvard University, bobbing his red head behind that mescal hummock. Pop Ginter complaining sourly as usual, but

131

secretly welcoming this moment of strife. Rocky Flint talking as he had to opponents in the ring: "Come on in. Come in and fight. Come in and get it!"

Dog-faced cavalry, thought Seaver proudly. As fine a bunch of fighting men as this world will ever know.

Bullets snarled in the brush and tore at the rocks, spraying them with barbed thorns and stone dust, and arrows slithered and clashed among the boulders. We could hold them off forever here, Seaver considered. But that's no good. We've got to drive on to Burnside. The whole campaign may hang on our getting back to the post.

The Apaches came in a sudden hurtling rush on horseback, and the Winchesters really opened up on them now, one hundred and eighty degrees of compact blazing fire that slashed down ponies and screeching braves in the weltering dust, turned the rest of them back and away. "They're crazy," Seaver said, spitting tobacco juice that tasted of powdersmoke. "Or else Monty found their main camp up there, and Hatchese has told 'em to keep us from gettin' back to the fort, no matter what it costs 'em."

The attackers had faded into the mist, as abruptly and completely as they had struck, leaving only their dead and wounded. A pony that screamed with a high human note until a .44 found it. A shirt-tailed buck who crawled like a broken-backed animal until Slats Dillon slammed a final shot into him. The rest were corpses or close enough to it. . . . Seaver passed the word to fall back on the picket line in that arroyo, and prepare to move out.

There were no casualties beyond splinter-flayed cheeks and slug-seared arms, Seaver learned with relief, as they gathered with the horses. But there would be later. . . . In the saddle, they moved out the southern end of the defile, as the sun rose blood-red above the eastern Peloncillos. That was the beginning of a long and hideous nightmare, a forced march under almost ceaseless enemy fire from the flanks and rear.

The sun soared higher in the molten blue, and the heat became barbarous, brutal in its intensity. Drenched in sweat, silted Confederate gray with dust, the column toiled on across the barren broken plains of Hellsgate toward the principal range of the Osages. Girths frothed white, saddle-leather scorched through uniform pants, rifle barrels burned the most calloused palms. Lips were parched and split to the texture of scar tissue, each lower one with its central gash, eased only by leaves of chewing tobacco. Eyes sank ever deeper into blackened, hollow-cheeked skulls of faces. Misery grew in the harassed ranks until death seemed almost welcome, if it could come in one quick flash.

They fought on horseback in the open glare, and on foot in the sparse shadow of rock clusters and monoliths and pitahaya shafts. The Apaches swooped in and out on their fleet ponies, or filtered in afoot through the salt cedars and boulders and hackberry. The drone of lead and the swish of arrows were constant things in the furnace heat.

Two pack horses were the first casualties, and Seaver handed out extra bandoleers of cartridges from them, saying: "They'll be killin' more horses. Wear all the extra shell belts you can stand, boys. May not be able to stop and get 'em later." With bandoleers slung over sunburnt shoulders and uniforms filthy and shredded, they looked more than ever like the bandits Cris Herrold said they resembled.

Then dour balding Pop Ginter caught an arrow clean through lungs and body, the barbed and feathered shaft protruding front and back. They hacked off the head and tugged it out, plugging the holes, but there wasn't much else they could do. "If they stuck to bows, they'd kill us all," Ginter growled, slow and labored. "Never learn — to shoot guns. . . . Shove along, damnit! What you waitin' here for?" But they waited for Pop Ginter to die, fighting off the enemy as they lingered there in a tangle of iron-wood, tarragon and sandstone outcroppings. The sound of his breathing was terrible, and it took a long time for it to end. . . . With Ginter wrapped in his blanket and lashed across the saddle, they went on under the blinding sun.

In the afternoon a rifle bullet struck the curly head of young Gus Karras, as he reached for a plug of tobacco from Tex Dallas. The Texan whirled and spotted the pallid muzzle-streak, hammered a lightning fast shot into that red sniper, and caught Gussy before he could topple from the saddle. There was no need to wait this time. They tied Karras on his horse and continued the march.

"They'll knock us all off, one by one," muttered Corporal Shiller.

"Cut it, Shill," said Seaver. "We're gettin' three and four to every one. Better'n that when they rush us. We're doin' all right."

Charley Crater laughed, teeth white in his lean grimed face. "You think we was comin' to a health camp out here, Shill?"

"Button your lip, you Kansas jayhawker!" rasped Shiller.

"That's better," grinned Crater. "That's the way to talk, Shill."

They stumbled on through that blazing inferno of sand and stone, eyeballs inflamed and distended, cracked lips bleeding, beard-stubble matted with the sweaty paste of alkali and powder, tongues swollen too large for their mouths, and throats clogged aching dry. Glances roving and ranging without rest, carbines always ready, they reeled on over the slow tortured miles, sun-dazed, sick and giddy, fighting off the furtive flitting shadows that clung leechlike on either flank. Fighting every foot of the endless way.

Toward evening, when the sun was dipping low in the west and the mountains were looming close before them, Cantey was hit as he stooped to pry a pebble from the shod hoof of his mount, one slug smashing his left shoulder, another piercing his throat. Cantey collapsed in a bright fountain of arterial blood, and they waited briefly for the life to bubble out of the strapping Irishman, whose fine tenor voice had entertained them so often in the barracks and in the field.

They slung him over the saddle and plodded forward, twenty men now where there had been twenty-three. Progress had been distressingly slow. At the rate they were going, Burnside was still four or five days away. If it keeps on like this, Seaver estimated gloomily, not one of us will ever reach the fort.

As twilight grayed into dusk, the column was moving along a ridge scattered with pines and junipers and brush-grown boulders, toward the entrance of Cadnac Cut. The Apaches launched another all-out assault, screaming in from either wing with fanatical fury, and for one horrible moment it looked as if the copper-skinned maniacs were going to sweep the ridgetop and overrun the detail.

But the cavalrymen, flinging from the saddle and firing as fast as they could line, trigger and lever the carbines, finally checked the red hordes and lashed them back on both sides. Horseholders controlled the mounts, and the fighters went to their Colt revolvers when the Winchesters were emptied. The attack was hurled back with heavy losses, and Seaver, his own rifle red-hot and his pistol smoking, thought: Now we'll make Cadnac Cut and over the hump into Chickasaw Pass. They can't get at us good until we're down and out on the other side of the mountains, but I'd better send a runner on ahead tonight.

Looking around in the smoke-blurred dusk beneath the pines, Seaver silently thanked God for soldiers like Shiller, Dillon, Dallas, Crater, Emmett and Flint. Like Thackston, Jarnigan, Hendree, Slocum, Zastrow, Parilli, O'Doul, and the others. . . . If a man had to die here, he died in good company.

Seaver started checking for casualties. Some of the horses were down in the brush. Stonesifer was swabbing and probing Lemonick's bared shoulder, and Ullrich was deftly bandaging Lafferty's thigh. Tex Dallas tried to dig a slug out of Flint's broken arm, and Rocky said, "With one hand I can lick anybody from Texas, and don't forget it." Emmett tenderly bathed a ragged crease in Fennell's red head, and Zastrow was wrapping Cockrell's bullet-raked hand.

For a minute Seaver thought gratefully that no further damage had been inflicted on his small force. Then he heard Crater cursing, and turned to see Charley standing over the long loose-sprawled frame of Slats Dillon, dead in a thicket of wild plums. . . . Many's the bottle I've emptied with that tall skinny Slats, thought Seaver, turning away and swearing hoarsely through the knot in his throat.

They re-formed and climbed on, nineteen left of their twenty-three, with forty or fifty Apaches still on their heels, and Burnside far away in the southeast. Entering the mouth of Cadnac Cut, they started the long uphill march toward the summit of the pass, with darkness closing in densely about them. Night and this narrow steep-walled corridor had saved them for another day, at least.

When they halted for late supper, Seaver announced that he wanted a volunteer courier to ride to Burnside. He was endeavoring to save, not only his own detail, but Montrill's party as well, providing they were still alive back there.

"That's me, Sarge," said young Bucky Thackston. "I'm the best rider with the fastest horse, and I've got interests to protect at the post, too. That Vermilya's holdin' two hundred dollars of mine, if he hasn't gambled and drunk it up already."

Seaver scrawled a message to Major Thurston, and gave the dark devil-may-care boy detailed verbal instructions.

"I'll hit Burnside tomorrow night," Bucky Thackston promised casually. "Have the whole force back here in a couple days. If

139

you can't hang on till then, you ain't worth savin'."

Thackston saddled his big dun gelding, waved a grinning farewell like a schoolboy off on a lark, and rode on up the mountain passage into the night.

The column mounted as far as possible in the Cut that night, horses and men dragging themselves wearily up the grade. Turning in then, they were exhausted enough to sleep in the highland chill, that bit through blankets and clothing into the marrow of aching bones. . . . They were up and climbing forward again at daybreak, fighting an almost continuous rear-guard action, as the Apaches closed up in the deep corridor, with the coming of light.

At the summit the cavalry paused to dig in, fort up, and smash the enemy back down the northern slope. Then, dropping into Chickasaw Pass, they descended southward in the direction of the Cherokee Valley, making better time in the upland coolness and shade, with the Indians restricted to the rear. If Thackston got through safely, they might hold out until they met the main force from Burnside. . . .

But that afternoon in the lower reaches of Chickasaw Pass, they came upon what remained of young Bucky Thackston, who must have run into some of Hatchese's scouts. It was a gruesome spectacle, grisly enough to turn the toughest campaigner away, gagging and retching and ill with horror. The Apaches had staked him out over a slow fire, eyes gouged out, ears lopped off, fingers and toes chopped away, the whole torso stenciled with cuts and seared with burns. The mutilated corpse was left dangling from an oak limb, so the column would be certain to see it.

That meant there would be no relief from Fort Burnside. The detail would have to fight its way home alone, step by step, and there were Indians ahead of them now, as well as behind. . . . Shocked with the sight of that hanging horror, Seaver and every man there looked death in the eye, felt its ghastly closeness, and tasted its evil breath.

They buried Thackston in a ferny pocket beside the trail, along with the other dead — Dillon, Cantey, Karras and Ginter. The odds were bad enough without trying to transport those bodies, and the horses were needed for the living. Their number was reduced to eighteen now.

They cleared the bottom of Chickasaw Pass in the waning red-hazed light of sunset, the western horizon a riot of flaming colors, threaded the lofty majestic Spires, and swung eastward for Redstone Butte and the headwaters of the Cherokee. The Apaches would be closing up from the rear, now that they were out in open country again, and more of the warriors were probably lurking somewhere in front of them.

Eighteen men and five of them wounded, not severely but enough to weaken them and impair their effectiveness in combat. Seaver could still feel and smell the awesome nearness of death.

CHAPTER XI

Montrill peered over the parapet of the basaltic rim and down a long sharp slope that was strewn with rocks and pinons, clumps of catclaw and mescal, and the red-brown bodies of dead Apaches. They had tried to storm this hillside twice, and it had been costly in the face of those Winchester repeaters. Now the sun was sinking in a carmined sea of colors beyond the westerly Osage peaks, but the heat lingered with heavy suffocating pressure, and the stone burned through Montrill's sweat-soaked uniform. He had never known such utter weariness. For five days they'd been on the run, hunted like rabbits by wolf-packs of Indians. It could not go on much longer. The whole countryside was alive and swarming with the warriors of Hatchese. Only the infinite knowledge and skill, the rare instincts and superlative woodcraft of Jim Raven had saved them thus far.

Montrill's eyes were a sunken bitter green, and bronze beard stubble covered his strong jaws and hollowed cheeks, above which the cheekbones stood out in angular prominence. His broad mouth was seared dry, with that central split in the lower lip. From time to time he moistened it with tobacco juice from his tongue. His tawny head and wide muscular shoulders sagged with exhaustion. The carbine was under his arm, the .44 Colt in its flapless holster, and an extra bandoleer of shells hung slanting across his chest. Montrill looked like a hard-fighting, battle-worn veteran ready for a last-ditch stand.

This position was secure, a natural pyramid rising several hundred feet above the surrounding scrub-wooded hills, topped by a stone-girded knob that was depressed in the center. The only approach lay before Montrill. The other three sides were sheer precipices, but there was a possibility of getting down the cliff at the rear. Jim Raven had charted a course, and they were going to attempt it under cover of darkness. If they got away, it would give them another day or two. . . . If relief didn't arrive from Burnside by that time, there was no hope anyway. The cause was lost, and so were they.

In the bowl behind Montrill, a thin stand

of paloverdes and stunted cedars shaded a tiny seep of water. Four horses were tethered under the trees, and the mortally wounded Dunleavy lay there suffering in silence. Ashley and Raven rested in the shade, while Montrill stood his watch at the front rim.

They hadn't escaped unscathed in these five days of grim hide-and-seek and savage running skirmishes. Corporal McCord had died down there two days ago, in the chaparral and mesquite-tangled labyrinth of a narrow dry wash. Shot through the broad chest and pinned down with a broken leg crushed under his dead horse, husky stolid McCord was alive, conscious, and begging them to shoot him. The Apaches were close on top of them at the time, and there was no chance of getting the dying man out of there.

"I'm a goner, damn it," McCord panted. "Shoot me. Don't leave me for them to finish. Dunny! You do it, Dunny!"

Dunleavy had dismounted and crouched beside him, while the other three fought off the Indians with blasting carbines. "Mac, I can't do it," Dunleavy said. "I *can't,* Mac. . . ."

"For Pete's sake, you got to!" moaned McCord. "Shoot me and get the hell outa here! I'd do it — for you, Dunny."

"I'll lug you out, Mac."

"The devil with that!" McCord sobbed through a bloody froth. "Kill me, for the love o' Mike, Dunny! Put me outa this, *please,* Dun! . . ."

It was the blood-lusting screech of the Apaches that finally convinced and prompted Dunleavy, steeled him to the task. "All right, Mac, look away," he groaned, drawing his revolver. "God bless you, boy!" His blackened, crag-jawed face ugly and distorted beyond belief, Dunleavy had shot his friend in the back of the head, mounted and plunged out of that barranca with the others, outrunning the pursuit when the warriors stopped to scalp and butcher McCord's lifeless body.

And now, two days later, Dunleavy himself was gutshot and dying, with a bullet in his abdomen.

On the steep dusky slope in front of Montrill, vultures flapped heavily down and settled raw-necked and greedy-beaked on the coppery bodies left behind from those crazed frontal attacks. The scavengers are devouring their own kind, thought Montrill. The evil carrion birds tear at the dead like Hatchese's bucks do. . . . And he was filled with a sudden overpowering hatred for the enemy that prowled the pine forests below the escarpment.

But Montrill was too spent to retain that feeling of hate for long. Nerves and sinews had been strained beyond the breaking point; the brain was as numb and drained as the body. Leaning on the wall, Montrill let his thoughts stray back into the faraway past. . . . Bright boyhood days with Lance and their sisters and Stuart Crowl at Montrill Manor. Odd, how often he dreamed of the place, as if it still stood gracious and serene, instead of being burned to ashes over ten years ago. The white-pillared veranda, honeysuckle and rambler-rose in the yard, the smell of Georgia pine and sun-warmed peaches . . . magnolia.

All the memories were sunlit or moon-gilded. Swimming in the yellow Chattahoochee, galloping the red clay roads, hunting in the smoky autumns, dancing at the Manor and Crowl House, Shepley Court, Ellinrude Hall, and Bordelais Terrace. The glittering scented ballrooms of Atlanta. The girls like lovely flowers. . . . Is it because I am going to die, that these thoughts come to me? wondered Montrill.

Life had held so much in those young days, and promised so much more. A magnificent thoroughbred called Cavalier, a girl named Vera Ellen in a wine-colored gown.

Amanda, who was still fire in the loins and a singing in the chest, to remember after all the years. . . . The poems of Byron, the taste of juleps. A pine-cone fire and a banjo tinkling and a hound baying the moon. . . . He would go to Virginia to study or perhaps V.M.I., and Lance would follow him there. It was all planned, but they went to war instead.

It wasn't much of a life, after that. The world they had known and loved was destroyed, wiped out entirely, the homes reeking cellarholes, the people dead or gone. Hopes and dreams shattered, none of the brave young promises fulfilled. . . . At thirty-two years it came to this: A bald knob of rock in the Southwest wilderness, surrounded by hostile savages.

Montrill smiled somberly, rubbed his hot brow with a grimy hand, and wet his cracked lips with tobacco juice. Night was coming fast, but if the Indians wanted them badly enough, they might even try to mount the slope in the darkness. They'd do anything for Hatchese, it seemed. Jim Raven had pointed out the chief himself that afternoon. Hatchese was big for an Apache, tall, broad and powerful, with a huge broken blade of a nose and a wide down-turned mouth. In all the heat, with most of his bucks stripped to the waist, Hatchese wore a faded blue army tunic with the shoulder bars of a captain. He had an immense and severe dignity, a solemn pomp and pride, that would have been absurd and laughable but for the power and menace embodied in the man.

Ashley emerged from the trees and climbed to the rimrock to relieve Montrill. His thin face was drawn to the bone, burnt to a crisp, the brown eyes receded, the cheeks and throat emaciated-looking. But Ashley still had a ghost of his friendly, pleasant smile. "How've they been behaving, Rick?"

'Quiet, Ash. But they might come up tonight. For Hatchese they'd risk dying at night and having their souls left in perpetual darkness."

"He's got something, that Indian," conceded Ashley. "Dunny wants to see you, Rick."

"Is he worse?"

Ashley nodded sadly. "Can't last much longer. Be a blessing for him to die, Rick. He's been in agony so long."

"And he wants to go," Montrill said, "since that business with McCord."

"I don't know what's kept any of us alive here."

"Jim Raven," said Montrill, with a slow grin.

"Yes, of course," Ashley agreed, smiling in response. "And if he gets us down that cliff, we should live forever."

Montrill spat an amber stream. "For a few more days anyway, Ash. Ought to see some reinforcements tomorrow or the next day, if Seav got the boys through to Burnside."

"Have to come soon, Rick. Can't live on chewing tobacco, water and gunpowder indefinitely."

"You don't mean you're hungry, Ash?" drawled Montrill.

Ashley laughed shortly. "I'm beyond that, boy. My stomach's shrunk so I couldn't eat a thing, even if we had something besides that jerky of Jim's."

Montrill cuffed his shoulder. "I'll go down and see Dunny."

Montrill walked stiffly down into the hollow, feeling old and cramped, brittle and empty.

Left alone at the parapet, Ashley contemplated the long and devious, yet fleeting path that had led him to this naked hilltop in Arizona Territory. Childhood in Vermont, the long sparkling sheen of Lake Champlain between the rolling Green Mountains and the jagged Adirondacks. Taste of maple sap in the spring, and the flare of maple leaves in the fall, white frozen winters with the ring of skates. College and the elms of New Haven, cut short by the war. Culp's Hill at Gettysburg, Lookout Mountain, the Wilderness, Cold Harbor. . . . Transfer to Sheridan's cavalry. . . . Opequan, Cedar Creek, and Five Forks.

Back to Yale after Appomattox, but no longer interested in book learning. So Ashley eventually re-enlisted, went west with the Third Cavalry, and was still a lieutenant. . . . And pretty close to being a dead lieutenant, he concluded wryly. With Montrill, a Rebel from Georgia, his best friend. . . . Funny, the tricks fate played on a man and his life and ambitions. Or was *funny* the correct word?

Montrill moved through the cedars and paloverdes, stretching out to drink from the spring and slosh water over his bronze head and face. Jim Raven was asleep, or pretending to be. Montrill sat down beside Sergeant Dunleavy, who was lying blanket-wrapped on a bed of moss. Dunleavy's bearded face had sunken until the great jaws and cheekbones jutted more than ever. His deep-hollowed eyes were feverish and anguished, but he tried to smile at Montrill. The odor from his wound was rank on the still twilight air.

"The stink ain't nice, Monty," he murmured weakly. "I'm used to it. But for you fellahs — it's bad."

"I'm sorry we couldn't do more for you, Dunny."

"Don't matter, Monty. You done all you could." Dunleavy moved his head. "Except what I did for Mac. Hardest thing — ever did."

"The best thing you could have done for him," Montrill said earnestly.

"Second white man I ever killed."

"Mac was dying. You didn't really kill Mac. You just saved him from torture, Dun."

"I did — the other one," panted Dunleavy. "Ain't got — much time, Monty. Wanta tell you. Been on — my mind — and conscience."

Montrill was beginning to suspect what was coming. "All right, Dunny," he said gently.

"It was me — that day over the Aravaipa." Dunleavy's gaunt features were ashen gray under the powderstains and dirt and tan. "Shot Dirk Herrold."

"Then you saved my life, Dunny. Or Seaver's."

"Couldn't let him — throw down — on

you and Seav." Dunleavy's head rolled on the pillowed blanket. A spasm of pain racked him, and sweat sprang out in large drops on his agonized face.

"He had it coming, Dunny," said Montrill. "Don't try to talk any more now. And don't worry about that. Or anything, Dun."

Dunleavy reached out one big hand, and Montrill clasped it firmly. "Goin' out, Monty. Feel it comin'. You boys — you'll make out fine. Now, Monty — rather be alone — now."

Montrill smiled understandingly and released Dunleavy's hand. Rising with a farewell gesture, Montrill turned and strode back to the little spring, his eyes scalded and grief clutching at his throat. The old soldier, knowing he wasn't going to die easy, wanted to fight it out by himself.

There was a threshing sound from the blankets, a terrible whimpering moan, and then silence. When Montrill looked around, it was all over. Sergeant Dunleavy was stark and dead on his back, that great fighting chin thrust up at the dimming sky.

It was better for all concerned, Montrill admitted with reluctance. Dunleavy was out of his hopeless torment, and they were free to run and fight and hide again, providing Raven could take them down that cliff in the rear. Montrill believed he would manage it somehow. After the last five days it was difficult to conceive an obstacle that Jim Raven couldn't overcome. The scout seemed endowed with supernatural powers.

Walking away to examine the picketed horses, Montrill thought of Anita Raven with sudden hope, warmth and hunger. Jim was right: he had been too lackadaisical with the girl. When they got back to Burnside — if they ever did — he was going to assert himself. Cut Herrold out, and take Nita for his own. Herrold would never marry her anyway. Not the half-breed daughter of an Indian scout. But Montrill would, and the devil with officers' row. That was what he wanted and needed. Montrill wondered why he had let so much time go to waste.

But Burnside was as remote as another planet to them, unless Major Thurston brought K and L troops up across the Osages and Hellsgate within the next few days.

CHAPTER XII

At Fort Burnside, a week had passed without any word from the patrol. The entire garrison, from the sutler's swamper to Major Thurston, from the squaws in the laundry to the major's daughter, was perturbed and fearful about the expedition. Rumors ran from post headquarters to the blacksmith shop, from officers' row to the barracks. It was discussed in the bakery and commissary, the stables and breaking corral, and by the men lined up on sick call at Dr. Halversen's fortess-like adobe hospital. The column had been cut to pieces in the Osage Mountains. . . . The detail had been annihilated on the Hellsgate. . . . Major Thurston was worried, because some dispatch should have been received within the week, but he refused to credit any such noxious gossip.

Time lagged and tension grew in the quadrangle, nerves were rubbed raw and wire-edged, tempers flared hot and quick. Jocular ribbing in the mess hall or on the parade led to rough-and-tumble brawls in the barracks and bare-knuckle fights behind the stables. The guardhouse, near the main gate, was well-populated during this period. Tough swaggering Sergeant Kirk, primed with whiskey and tired of playing peace-maker, lashed out with his own lightning fists at Corporal Magill and Private High-tower. Those three landed in the brig with the other miscreants, some of whom Kirk had turned in previously.

The stress and pressure, amplified by monotony, told on Crispin Herrold as much as anyone. Trapped at his desk in the post adjutant's office, feeling left out, unwanted and disgraced in this non-combatant role, Herrold fretted and chafed and cursed the interminable paper work, the unvarying routine; and watched Barron drill platoons from K and L, until they were on the verge of dropping in the cruel heat. The arm-chair general seemed to take a sadistic delight in that, and Herrold wanted more than ever to challenge Barron. In other moments, Her-rold was tempted to ride over to the For-rester ranch, call Kirby Tisdale out, and shoot him dead. . . . Anything for action, excitement, release from this stultifying boredom.

This afternoon, having drilled a platoon from L into a blind sun-stricken stupor on the heat-blasted parade, Ray Barron retired to his single adobe for a bath and a change. Dressed in fresh uniform trousers and shirt, Barron slicked his neutral-colored hair into a shining cap and studied his broad aquiline-nosed face in the mirror. An idea, spawned by desire, had been formulating in his brain. With Montrill and Jim Raven gone, and Herrold concentrating his attentions on Tess Thurston, Anita Raven was alone most of the time.

Buttoning his tunic and adjusting his carefully creased campaign hat, Barron stepped out into the fading afternoon, crossed the parade, and turned toward the hospital on its slight rise at the end of the rectangle. Stopping at the sutler's, he bought a pint of the better whiskey. That might help, although it probably wouldn't be necessary. With a deep quiver inside him, a quickening of the pulse, Barron thought of that tawny tigress of a Creole in New Orleans. Those wenches of mixed blood were passionate, unrestrained and wanton.

Walking past the hospital, Barron turned left in the shadow of the stockade, pausing as if to inspect the sentry post at the gate in this far southern wall, then tramping on toward the log cabin in the opposite corner. Smartly uniformed, square and erect, a man of dignity and wilful assurance. There was no doubt in his mind that both Montrill and Herrold had enjoyed the favors of Anita Raven. A female of her status had little other reason for existing. Barron saw no point in denying himself this pleasure any longer.

Anita Raven came to the door as he approached, masking her surprise and another expression that Barron couldn't quite fathom. She evidently had been cleaning house. A gay bandanna was tied about her glossy blue-black hair, the sleeves were rolled high on her firm rounded arms, and faint perspiration glistened on her cameo-clear face. Her legs were bare under the skirt, her skin a rich dark golden brown, smooth and flawless. High-breasted, slim of waist, and superbly hipped, she had a full-curved figure of flowing grace that caused Barron to catch his breath.

"Aren't you out of bounds, Lieutenant?" asked Anita Raven, with the barest trace of an accent.

"Just making the rounds, Anita. Aren't you going to ask me in?"

"This *is* out of bounds — for staff officers."

Barron smiled wisely. "But not for a certain pair?"

"Old friends," she said, laughing lightly, "are welcome. On invitation."

"New friends can be nice, too," Barron said. "I thought you might be getting lonesome, Anita."

"Why?"

"Well, your father's away, and Montrill. . . . And Herrold seems to have found other interests."

"I don't mind being alone, Mr. Barron," said Anita. "If you'll excuse me, I have some work to finish."

Barron stepped a stride closer. "I am lonely, Anita, and I admit it. Please let me come in and mix a drink. I have some whiskey, but I prefer water with it."

"Why, I didn't suppose you drank, Mr. Barron." The girl smiled and shook her fine dark head. "All right — for one drink."

Anita Raven turned inside and Barron followed, watching the sway of her splendid hips. "It's very pleasant here," he remarked, surprised at the neatness and comfort of the place.

"Sit down, please. I'll get the water and a glass. . . . No, I don't care for it myself. But you must be tired, after that hard drill."

Barron sensed rather than heard the shade

of mockery. "Have to keep them fit, Anita. It's rough on the boys, but it may save their lives sometime, out in the field."

"For their own good," Anita murmured. "That's fine . . . unless they drop dead some day on the parade!" She placed a glass and pitcher of water on the table.

Barron was annoyed, angered, but he disliked to spoil what he considered a good beginning. "I know, Anita. It's hard for you ladies to understand. . . . I wish you'd join me." He mixed water with whiskey and raised the glass in a gallant flourish. "To your rare dark beauty!"

"Thank you." She was moving around with effortless ease, straightening chairs and bright Navajo rugs, and Barron watched her admiringly.

"Sit down and talk with me, Anita."

"Sorry, but I'll have to ask you to leave, Mr. Barron."

There was tacit contempt in everything she said to him, and real anger roared up in Barron. Draining the glass, he stood up, his bulk wide and stiff. "Apparently you don't consider me the equal of Herrold and Montrill."

"It's not that at all," she protested.

"What is it then?" Barron demanded, moving toward her. No half-breed jade was going to give him this kind of treatment.

Anita Raven backed away, but there was no fear in her great gray eyes and calm serene face. "Please go now. You're a West Pointer and a gentleman."

Ray Barron advanced, arms half-lifted to grasp her rounded figure, but Anita Raven had backed to Jim's gun rack by this time. Lifting a long-barreled pistol, she cocked and lined it with swift practiced precision. "Get out!" Her voice was a whiplash across his blood-swollen countenance. "And don't ever come back!"

Barron's hands dropped, his heavy form slumping. "I'm sorry, Anita. You're so lovely, I lost my head for a minute. Please forgive me."

"You don't need my forgiveness. I know what you think of me. Just go."

Barron gestured in palm-spread hopelessness, picked up his hat and bottle, and stomped out the door, turning at once toward officers' row. Anita Raven, the gun still hanging in her hand, crossed to the doorway and looked after him with cold gray eyes. . . . He rates me even lower than Cris Herrold does, she thought with bitter wisdom. Only Rick Montrill considers me a lady. I never fully appreciated Rick, the finest gentleman of them all. Perhaps when he

comes back . . . She gazed into the north-
west, where sunset colors were spreading
lavishly over the Osages, and wondered if
Rick Montrill and her father and the rest
would ever return to Burnside.

As Barron stalked in along the duckboards
of the row, Herrold came from the direction
of headquarters toward his 'dobe. They
would have met but neither wanted to, Barron slowing his stride, Herrold quickening
his to turn into his entrance. When Barron
reached it, still smarting and raging from
his encounter with Anita Raven, some
contrary impulse stopped him short on the
slat walk. Wanting to hurt both Herrold and
Montrill, he wheeled in to the former's
doorway, asking: "Want a drink, Cris?"

"I've got to clean up and shave," Herrold
said. "Thanks just the same."

"All right, boy." Barron started to back
out, then halted. "You want to know who
shot your brother, don't you?"

Herrold, pulling off his shirt, shrugged his
shoulders. "I'll find out sometime, Barron."

Barron laughed. "Everybody else knows
it, so you might as well."

"Well, let's have it." Herrold's tone and
look were impatient.

"Rick Montrill."

162

Herrold grimaced. "I've heard that rumor before."

"It's the truth, mister," said Barron. "Rick's brother Lance was down there on the Aravaipa, getting slaughtered with the rest. When Derrick Herrold refused to order his command into action, Rick Montrill killed him."

"You weren't there, Barron."

"I got it straight, just the same," Barron insisted. "Take it or leave it, Herrold; that's the way it happened."

"Thanks," Herrold said dryly, dismissal in his voice and expression.

"For nothing," added Barron, halfway out the door. "You wouldn't call Montrill for it anyway, mister. Somebody else perhaps, but not Montrill." He saluted mockingly, and left Herrold staring narrowly after him.

Spotting Teresa Thurston under the ramada of the commanding officer's house at the head of the row, Barron passed his own quarters and drew up before the blonde girl with a courtly bow. "Invite me in for an appetizer, Tess. I'm carrying the plunder." He tapped the concealed bottle.

"I'm expecting Cris, Ray," she said doubtfully.

"That's all right; he can have one with us," Barron declared jovially. "There's time

163

before retreat."

"Well, I could stand one," Teresa Thurston admitted. "And Dad's still at headquarters. . . . Come in, Ray. I've worried myself sick and frantic over that patrol."

Barron trailed her inside, laughing. "No need of worrying over a detail commanded by Montrill and Ashley, my dear young lady!"

Her dark blue eyes flickered sharply at him. "Heavy sarcasm doesn't become you, Lieutenant."

"Sorry, Tess; I didn't mean it that way," Barron apologized, wondering why everyone instantly resented him and his words.

Teresa Thurston laughed and clung to his arm. "That's all right, Ray. I'm a little nervy and upset, I guess."

They were flirting mildly over their glasses, when Crispin Herrold rapped and entered, shining clean and handsome, not at all pleased to discover his fellow officer's presence. Barron rose and reached for the whiskey. "I'm pouring this afternoon, Cris. You'll have that drink now, I trust."

"No thinks, Barron. I have something to say to Tess — in private."

"It can't be that urgent," Barron said. "Have a chair and I'll do the honors, Herrold."

"Don't bother," Herrold said curtly. "We can do without you and your bottle, Mr. Barron."

"*Cris!*" Teresa rose anxiously and stood before Herrold.

"You forget yourself *and* your manners, sir!" protested Barron, bridling with righteous indignation, his bold features suffused with choleric fire. He set bottle and glass down with a thud.

"I *shall* forget myself," Herrold warned, "if you don't clear out of here!"

"What's the matter with you, Cris?" asked Teresa. "Have a drink with us, and you'll feel better."

"I'll be all right — after he leaves."

A slight sneer twisted Barron's thin lips. "I'm not under your command, mister. And I'm not leaving!"

Everything so long pent up in Herrold exploded with a sudden white-hot flare. Thrusting past Teresa, he took one stride and swung his left hand, palm open, at that broad mottled face. He didn't realize what he had done until the tingle of it ran up his wrist and forearm, the loud smacking sound in his ears. Barron's sleek head rocked sidewise, and a startled gasping cry came from Teresa Thurston.

Grunting with shock and anger, Barron

recovered and threw his brawny bulk forward, swinging in ponderous might. Herrold's hands were up as he backed ducking away, taking most of them on arms, shoulders and skull. But Barron kept driving, finally beating down Herrold's guard and smashing the sides of his face with wicked hooking power. Herrold's shoulders slammed the solid adobe wall, jarring him from head to heels. The breath whistled from his lungs, and lights flashed behind his eyeballs. The warm salty taste of blood filled his mouth.

Barron crowded in, grinding Herrold against the 'dobe and slugging both big fists low into the body. Then, stepping back to set himself for the knockout, Barron's hands cocked low and wide, leaving him open. Herrold flung himself forward off the wall, firing left and right with terrific speed and explosive strength. Barron's head bobbed and jerked violently, the pomaded hair flying awry in stiff broken strands, as Herrold whipped him backward across the room, upsetting the table and other furniture. The tinkling glass and splintering wood were muted beneath the solid jolting impacts of Herrold's swift punching.

Barron bounced off the wall, and Herrold caught him with a lashing left, ripped him with the right. Barron hung there on jacking knees, eyes slashed blind and face streaming scarlet, arms dangling and helpless. Herrold straightened him with a spearing left, and threw the right hand with every coordinated ounce he could pour into the blow. It struck with shattering sound and force, like a meat-ax on the chopping block. Blood spattered and Barron stiffened upright beyond his normal height. Tottering on splayed legs then, Barron pawed the air, spun a top-heavy half-circle, and collapsed headlong with a jarring crash, face down and senseless on the pine floor.

Herrold was crouched tigerlike over him, panting and bleeding, with hands ready to strike again if necessary, when he became aware of another presence. Straightening and turning, lowering his raw-knuckled fists, Herrold saw Major Thurston standing in the doorway, red-faced and stern, his cigar at a menacing angle under the gray mustache.

"Very pretty!" he said. "Quite the proper way for officers and gentlemen to entertain a young lady. Tess, go to your room. Mr. Herrold, you are under arrest. Report to the corporal of the guard."

"Won't my quarters do, sir?"

"The guardhouse will do better," Thurston said. "At once, Herrold!"

"Yes, sir. But —" Herrold groped desperately.

"But nothing, mister!" cut in the major. "You threatened Mr. Barron recently. Now you have carried out that threat — in part, at least. You'll stand court-martial for this. Now report to the guardhouse!"

Chapter XIII

And that is where Lieutenant Crispin Herrold was the following afternoon — in the officers' block of the adobe jailhouse — when the ragged remnant of Seaver's column dragged itself home at last, escorted by a relief detail in the command of Shaddock. Gripping the rusted iron bars until his arms ached numbly to the elbows, Herrold watched them straggle in the main gate at the northeast corner of the stockade. . . . Eight days after their departure from their fort. Late afternoon, at about the time Dunleavy was dying on that rocky knob beyond Hellsgate Heights, between Castle Rock and Three Chiefs.

Fifteen men and a dozen horses. Battered scarecrows, blackened by sun and dirt and gunpowder, their uniforms hanging in filthy bloodstained tatters, grimy reddened bandages marking most of them, in one place or another. Eyes sunken out of sight in gaunt whiskered faces. Heads drooping, shoulders slumped, knees sagging, and worn-out boots shuffling, stumbling. . . . The horses fit to be shot, carrying the more seriously wounded and the dead. Three blanket-rolled corpses strapped across saddles. They had lost three more between The Spires and Redstone Butte: O'Doul, Cockrell and Corporal Shiller.

Fifteen left out of twenty-three, the survivors preserved by a series of miracles, and more dead than alive. Old Sergeant Seaver, the only officer among them, hobbling and aged but still indomitable. Whiplike Tex Dallas and rawhide tough Charley Crater. Little Tut Jarnigan and hulking Ox Hendree. The blond Ullrich and the good-looking Stonesfier. These seemed to be among the least injured.

Lafferty was limping with his carbine for a crutch, and Rocky Flint wore his arm in a crusted sling. Fennell's red head and Lemonick's stalwart shoulder were swathed in smeared rags. Emmett, tied in his saddle, showed more bandages than uniform. Silk Slocum was unconscious on a litter slung between two horses. Parilli had a leg wound, and Zastrow was delirious and raving with two bullets in his body.

They all had the haunted look of men who

had lived through hell, and would never be touched by anything again. Men beyond everything but death itself.

Seaver reported to Major Thurston, and delivered Montrill's written communication and map. "They was on us all the way back," Seaver said. "Never saw 'em hang so tight and long. We'd all be under, if Shaddock hadn't met us east of Redstone."

"Do you think it's possible that Montrill's party has survived?" inquired Thurston.

"Possible, maybe. Some of 'em might of lasted this far. But they can't hold out much longer, unless you get to 'em, Major."

"I'm marching with two troops tomorrow morning," Thurston said. "Sergeant, you did well to get any of them back here. Report to the hospital with the rest of your detail."

"I ain't hurt, Major," grumbled Seaver.

"You're all being hospitalized immediately."

"About tomorrow, sir?"

"You'll stay here with the force left to defend the post," Thurston told him gently. "Get along to the hospital, Seaver. You can use a bath, shave, and some rest in bed, I think."

Seaver grinned and spat tobacco juice. "Male nurses though, Major." He shambled wearily off, wagging his grizzled head.

With Seaver's column in Dr. Halvorsen's care, and Shaddock's detail dismissed, Thurston went into a conference with his staff at headquarters. The story drifted back piecemeal to the guardhouse. Eight known dead, and the rest practically stretcher cases. Pop Ginter, Gussy Karras, Slats Dillon, and the singing Cantey on Hellsgate. Bucky Thackston in the Osage pass. Corporal Shiller and Cockrell and O'Doul out beyond Redstone Butte. . . . K and L troops going out in the morning.

Retreat, guard mount, and evening mess. The hour call hollered from sentry post to post in the humid darkness. Tattoo was sounding across the light-and-shadow-patterned rectangle when Teresa Thurston appeared before the bars of Herrold's cell. He rose from the bunk and came forward, clutching the bars until his knuckles stood out bone-white under the abrasions.

"Tess, I've got to go tomorrow," Herrold said, with urgent intensity. "Tell the major he can strip my rank. I'll go as a trooper, I'll do anything, Tess. But I've got to go with them in the morning!"

"I'll tell him, Cris. But it won't do a bit of good, you know."

"He needs every man he can put in the field."

"But he won't empty the guardhouse, Crispin."

"What's he leaving behind — besides prisoners?"

"Not much, Cris," said Teresa. "Just a skeleton force, with the wounded and sick. Barron in command of the post."

"Barron! If there were any justice, Barron would be under arrest too." Herrold's aristocratic face crinkled in disgust.

"You started it, Cris."

"He provoked me deliberately. He's been baiting me for some time. And he reports me for threatening him!"

"It's too bad, Cris," said Teresa Thurston. "But Dad's doing what he considers right."

"Ask him anyway, Tess. Tell him I'll ride in the ranks."

The girl nodded. "I'll do the best I can, Crispin. I wish he weren't so busy planning the campaign. But I'll try, Cris."

She left, and Herrold moaned like a man in mortal agony. This was too much, more than he could endure. To be locked up like a criminal, with the biggest Indian battle in years coming up. His last chance to prove himself, redeem himself and clear the name of Herrold, was gone now, irrevocably lost. . . . He really was in disgrace here. This was the final failure, the ultimate defeat, the depths of degradation.

As soon as Teresa could gain an audience with her harried father, she mentioned Herrold's request, adding a plea of her own about how much it meant to the boy. And how much this boy meant to her. . . . But Major Thurston shook his gray head impatiently. "I'm sorry, Tess. I can't let him go, and he's soldier enough to know it. A man facing court-martial is in no position to be asking favors of his commanding officer." That was his final word on the subject.

Teresa Thurston returned to Herrold with the verdict. He turned away, flung himself face down on the bunk, and would not look at her or speak to her again. After waiting and pleading a few desolate minutes, Tess hastened away in the darkness.

Burnside bustled with brisk activity in the night, and excitement ran high and strong within the walls. The captains Jepson and Trible displayed more energy than they had in months. Jepson shook off his lethargy, with a flash of his old-time fire and spirit, and Treble shed his fretful nervousness. The troopers said old Treb was so glad to be getting away from his wife's tongue that he didn't care a hoot how many warriors

Hatchese had.

The quartermaster was busy checking out supplies and clothing, blankets and equipment replacements. In the stables, horses and saddle gear, wagons and harnesses, were inspected with minutest care. In the barracks, troopers of K and L repaired and saddle-soaped worn boots, belts and holsters, or oiled and kneaded softness into new items. Cleaned and checked guns, ammunition, canteens and knives. Wrote letters home to families, wives or sweethearts. And in some instances, the practical-minded or pessimistic made out crude last wills and testaments.

"Bucky Thackston left me two hundred dollars," Vermilya said. "Now I got to go out and get myself killed before I can spend it. Ain't that a helluva note though?"

"Bucky had a furlough comin' next month," said Audette.

"O'Doul's enlistment was up in a coupla weeks," Sulima remarked. "That's when they get it."

"I sure hope McCord lives through it," put in Gilkeson. "Mac still owes me three hundred from that time in St. Louis."

Vermilya laughed. "Mac'll never have three hundred, if he lives to be ninety-eight. You can cross that off, Gil."

"Why don't you will me that two hundred of Bucky's then, Vermin?"

"Not by a damn sight," said Vermilya. "That goes to my old lady, if I should stop one and lose my pretty hair."

"Them Indians won't fight, when they see us out in full force," Turco ventured, with mixed bravado and hope.

"The devil they won't, Turk!" scoffed Meskill. "Seaver says they're fired up enough to fight the whole United States Army."

Vermilya laughed. "Kirk's all burnt up about missin' this one. He's liable to bust outa that guardhouse."

"They say young Herrold's cryin' like a baby in there, 'cause he can't get out and go with us." Sulima shook his head. "Me, I'd just soon be in where he is."

"They oughta let him go and get knocked off," Vermilya said. "He and his family's got enough of us dog-faces killed."

"Is it true, young Hellfire batted Barron's brains out?"

"Somebody sure did, from the looks of Barron's pan," laughed Vermilya. "But I never thought that Herrold could lick a sick Mexican."

"You think Montrill's bunch can still be alive?"

"For my money, there ain't enough Apaches to down them five," declared Vermilya. "Monty and Jim and Ash, Mac and Dunny."

"They ain't superhuman," protested Sulima.

"Brother, they're as close to it as you're ever goin' to see," Vermilya said. . . .

The lamps burned late at headquarters, and Barron was painfully conscious of his battered face. In hospital beds Seaver's detail slept and woke on the verge of screaming, sweaty and shivering, to sleep fitfully again. In the Raven cabin, Anita knelt and prayed for her father and Rick Montrill and all of Burnside. . . . Teresa finally cried herself to sleep in the Thurston adobe.

Behind the bars in the enlisted men's block of the guardhouse, Sergeant Kirk, drunk on whiskey smuggled to him from the sutler's, howled at the moon like a curly wolf, heedless to the threats of fellow-inmates and guards. In the officer's section, Cris Herrold lay silent and sleepless, deaf to the adjacent uproar, staring sightlessly into starry space.

The racket subsided when orders came straight from the C.O. to release Sergeant Kirk, and to see that he was sober and fit for active duty by daybreak — if the guard detail had to douse him in the Cherokee River. Kirk, sobering instantly, said: "It was them bars makin' me loony." He glanced back at the other prisoners. "I'm crazy and you boys are smart, huh? So be it, then."

Short of non-coms, they had to have Kirk tomorrow. There was an even greater dearth of commissioned officers, but they didn't want or need Lieutenant Crispin Herrold. . . . He was thinking of Montrill now, fixing the blame for all his misfortune on the Southerner. It probably was Montrill who had shot his brother Dirk. Montrill had more reason to than anyone else that particular day. Always that big quiet easygoing Rebel. . . . Herrold calmly decided that he would have to kill Montrill, if Rick ever got back here alive.

In the morning before sunrise the troopers came out with their mounts and formed on the parade, with chill white mists from the Cherokee drifting through the ranks. Two troops in full field equipment with escort wagons and pack train, rations and forage for fifteen days. Major Thurston himself in command, Jepson to head K and Trible leading L, Shaddock in charge of the escort train. Complete with color guard, guidons, trumpeters, and Indian scouts. The largest force ever to take the field from Burnside.

Teresa Thurston watched from her porch at the head of officers' row, and Barron stood on the duckboards at headquarters. Anita Raven stepped out of the log house beyond the row. Seaver and other unwounded members of his detail looked on from the hospital in the southwest corner. The skeleton force remaining behind was gathered in front of the barracks, and prisoners peered through the guardhouse grill.

Hanging on the cold flaky iron bars, Cris Herrold observed this brave and stirring scene, with sickness in the pit of his stomach, despair in his heart and soul. Commands rang out in the fog, and there was the smash of bodies striking leather as they mounted, the jangle and clash of metal equipment. They moved out the main gate in a long double file, dust rising in the morning mist, colors and guidons fluttering, the tramp of hoofs jarring the damp earth, escort wagons rumbling in the rear.

The rust-pocked bars were cutting into Herrold's palms, but he was unaware of it, as of the hot tears that brimmed and blurred his vision. Some of those men were going to die, but that was better than being left behind in disgrace and confinement. In his desolation and disgust, Herrold envied them all . . . even those who would not be coming back.

Chapter XIV

Montrill sighed and stirred in his blanket on the packed-earth floor, waking from another dream of sun-splashed Montrill Manor on the lazy-flowing Chattahoochee. He had seen his tall gravely handsome father, his mother with her sad sweet smile, and Lance laughing, his bright head thrown back, Clarice and Gail demure in the background, all as plain as day. And tasted that delicious baked ham from the smokehouse. . . . Awake now, he was miserable, chilled, the mountain cold aching in his weary bones. In a crumbling cabin, rank with mould and the sweat of horses and men, dark except for the moonlight that filtered down through pine boughs and touched Ashley in the doorway, carbine across his bony knees.

"Can't you sleep, Rick?" inquired Ashley, turning his keen profile.

"Too tired, Ash."

The slim New Englander laughed. "Too tired to sleep, too starved to eat. We're in a heck of a fix!"

"Jim ought to be back," Montrill said.

"He'll be coming. You can't hear him until he's beside you."

Montrill yawned and scratched the itching bristles on his lean jaws, wondering what it would be like to be clean again, shaved and bathed, in fresh laundered clothes, rested and comfortable. A dream, as far off as Georgia.

Three more days of fantastic flight, running fights, narrow escapes, and breathless hiding, had gone by since Dunleavy died on that rocky summit. High in the mountains toward Three Chiefs, east of Hellsgate and Castle Rock, they had taken shelter in this abandoned hut, which Jim Raven said had once belonged to Pete Magner. . . . The night after Dunleavy's death, Jim had piloted them down that cliff without mishap. The next day Ashley's chestnut mare was shot from under him, but fortunately he had Dunleavy's rawboned roan to switch onto. Somehow they were still ahead of the Apaches, but that kind of luck was bound to run out before long.

They were weakened by exhaustion and lack of nourishment, having eaten nothing but hardtack and jerked beef for days. They were worn out from endless strain and tension, the fatigue of constant battle. Jim Raven's long black hair had grayed noticeably in the past few days. Ashley and Montrill had aged until they looked like old men of twice their years. The limit was almost reached, and they all knew it. One more day was about all they could hope for.

Montrill got up and paced the dirt floor to restore circulation, working his arms and shoulders, lifting his knees high. Shaping and lighting a cigarette with numb fingers, he leaned on the door jamb over the seated Ashley. "I guess my plan was a poor one, Ash."

"It might work out yet, Rick."

"They'll have to come tomorrow then."

"I had a dream," Ashley murmured. "Saw them coming, Rick, two full troops. . . . Maybe it'll come true — tomorrow."

Jim Raven returned from his lone scout, and squatted before them. "Hills are crawlin' with Injuns. Thicker'n ticks on a sheep. Maybe we oughta hit that shortcut back to Burnside."

"Have to, Jim," agreed Montrill, "if the cavalry doesn't come by tomorrow."

"Start swingin' that way in the mornin'," Raven said. "Horses can't take much more.

Neither can we."

"Did you hear anything, Jim?"

"A lot of braggin' about wipin' out Seaver's whole bunch. I don't put much stock in it. Most likely they picked off a few of 'em. Injuns always lie when it comes to countin' coups."

"Is it safe to sleep here, Jim?" asked Ashley.

"Safe as anywhere, boys. They won't move till mornin'. We'll pull out early." Raven rose and stretched to his full lanky height. "We sure been lucky, boys. Never saw such luck. . . . Had us trapped twenty times, and there was always some kinda hole to crawl out of. A cut here, a canyon there, somethin' openin' up for us."

"It wasn't all luck, Jim," said Montrill.

"Well, mostly," Raven insisted. "Ninety per cent luck, Monty."

Montrill smiled and shook his head. "I'll sit up awhile now."

Ashley handed him the carbine and went inside, followed soon after by Raven. The horses could be heard shifting and chomping by the far wall. Montrill sat down in the doorway, the Winchester across his long thighs, and watched moonbeams splinter through the pines, while aspens rippled with pure silver fire in the breeze. After a few minutes, Raven came back and hunkered down beside him, hawk-face bleak and brooding.

"Monty, I been wantin' to ask you. If anythin' happens to go wrong, Monty . . . well, you'll kinda look after Nita, won't you?"

"I sure will, Jim. If she gives me the chance — instead of Herrold."

Raven snorted. "He's no account, Monty. Nita'll come to her senses and see that. . . . She's a fine girl, Monty. She would of been a great lady, if her mother had lived — to bring her up right."

"She *is* a great lady, Jim," said Montrill, with quiet sincerity.

"Well, I want you to look out for her anyway, son."

"Sure, Jim. But nothing's going to go wrong."

Jim Raven smiled inscrutably. "Maybe not, Monty. But it ain't natural for a man to be as lucky as I been lately. . . . Good night, son."

He returned to his blanket, and Montrill stared into the night with troubled eyes. Jim must have a premonition of death. No doubt they all did. Montrill had been thinking and dreaming more than ever of his boyhood home, the good times and people that were gone. And Ashley was talking more than usual about his family and summers in Vermont. Nearing the end of the road, men always looked back on the folks and places they had loved best. And these three had been hanging on at trail's end for eight long days since Castle Rock, eleven days out of Burnside. . . .

In the morning they were up before dawn, shuddering in the cold gray vapors, more spent and tired than ever. Rinsing their dry mouths with water, and swallowing a little. Trying to chew some more of Jim's jerked beef, washing the rubbery stuff down with water. Every move was an effort, every nerve and muscle in them cried out in protest against another day of this. The meat was like solid lead in their shriveled stomachs. Jim Raven eyed his plug of tobacco mournfully, shook his head, and put it back in the pocket of his buckskin shirt.

"When I can't take my mornin' chew, I know I'm pretty bad off," he said.

Their breath plumed smokily on the thin air, and Montrill dreaded the splitting agony of the first contact with stiffened saddle leather. They mounted like old rheumatic men, setting their teeth and driving the horses on up the mountainside where mist shrouded the pines. Saddles warmed and softened, the riders' joints loosening, their sinews becoming more responsive and pliable. Half an hour out of camp, they were awake and alive once more.

The sun rose like a flaming ball over the distant Peloncillos, its level rays shredding the fog and clearing the slopes, burning the dew off turf, pine needles and leaves. The horsemen wound and climbed for two hours, following rocky ledges, escarpments and deer runs in places, to confuse the pursuit. Or leaving a westward spoor and doubling back to the east along flinty ridgetops. At a gushing creek they watered the horses and themselves, replenished their canteens and washed up a bit, then splashed along the stream bed for a mile or more, to conceal their tracks. And always their necks were craning to watch the back trail, their hands ready to grasp carbines.

The general course had been northerly, but now Jim Raven swung a wide arc eastward and circled back to the south and west. This would bring them back to the eastern rim of Hellsgate, or take them to the cut-off Jim knew through the Osages. The most direct way back to Burnside, but no good for a column of any size. Raven had described and mapped the route for them, indicative again of his premonition.

They hoped to outflank their pursuers,

but anywhere in these wild uplands they were apt to run into Apaches. Hatchese had his warriors out in widely scattered packs, scouring the slopes and beating the brush for this tiny daring patrol that had defied them for a week.

Toward noon the terrain was dropping in long sweeping slants, the giant Douglas firs and ponderosa pines dwindling to ash and poplar, locust, birch and juniper. From vantage points, they could see the scorched broken jumble of Hellsgate stretching into the west, Castle Rock on the north, the backbone of the Osages to the south. With the field-glasses Montrill could make out roving bands of Indians in the wasteland, but there was no sign of the army.

"Looks like we've shook 'em off this trip," Jim Raven remarked. "First day they ain't been breathin' and shootin' down our necks." He grinned and tapped the butt of his booted carbine. " 'Course the day ain't over yet."

By mid-afternoon they were on a high yellow tabletop, studded with boulders and laced with desert vegetation, overlooking Hellsgate and not far from Castle Rock, where this mad chase had started. "This is where we make up our minds, boys," Jim

Raven announced. "Back into that hellhole down there, or over the mountains to the Cherokee." The decision wasn't difficult to arrive at. None of them wanted to plunge back into that maelstrom of Indians. They'd had enough, more than enough.

"Hold on, what's that?" Raven muttered, as they were about to turn back from the plateau rim and head for the short-cut.

At first it was just dust, clouding up in three distinct streamers from the choppy blistered surface of Hellsgate, moving north toward Castle Rock. Then the sound of gunfire rolled up to them, chattering furiously, fading off, and breaking out again. Apache patrols, flushed from arid ravines and arroyos, were fleeing northward, throwing shots back as they went. Now the blue-uniformed columns emerged in the smoking dust, a beautiful and unforgettable sight to the three men on the rimrock. Montrill felt his heart lift, his spine quiver, and his throat choke up with emotion. The Third Cavalry had come up at last.

The high-powered glasses brought it up close and clear, even though Montrill's eyes were stinging strangely, and the pattern of battle took shape and direction. A widespread three-pronged advance of army blue, sweeping the desert toward the monstrous towered butte at the north. Captain Trible on the near eastern wing. Major Thurston and Shaddock in the center. Captain Jepson commanding the far western flank. But where was Cris Herrold, back with the escort wagons? Or left behind altogether, as post adjutant at Burnside?

Montrill passed the binoculars on. Ashley said: "Isn't that wonderful? I'd like to be down there with 'em, the odds evened up for once!" Jim Raven had his look, and breathed almost reverently: "By God! We ain't been wastin' all our time at that, boys. Look at 'em go! Hatchese won't stand against the cavalry today."

Routed from the barrancas and potholes, leaving brown bodies scattered in the stone columns and brush, the Indians were in full flight. Other bands streamed down from the northeast hills to join them, milling about at the base of Castle Rock. There were brisk skirmishes on either wing, but the savages couldn't hold against the troopers. Thurston was hanging back in the middle, waiting for Jepson and Trible to clear the flanks and close in. Backed to the wall, the Apaches were caught in that well-timed and coordinated pincer movement.

"I guess the Old Man hasn't forgotten how," Montrill said, grinning happily. "And little Trib and fat Jep are earning their pay today."

"Hatchese isn't there," Ashley said, using the glasses again.

"A lot of 'em ain't there," Raven muttered, taking his turn. "Not much more'n a hundred penned in there. I thought they wasn't fightin' like they still do for Hatchese."

"Must be a hundred still in the mountains after us," Montrill estimated.

"That still leaves a main force with Hatchese," said Raven. "I don't like it, boys. They'll be hittin' from somewhere."

But the battle before them continued to claim their attention, with the climax approaching. Hooked in and pinned down from either side, the Apaches were a disorderly red rabble, howling in crazed defiance as they died under the murderous crossfire of the Winchesters, boiling aimlessly about the foot of the cliff, a chaos of panic, confusion and dense ruddy amber dust. Without Hatchese they were lost.

Major Thurston launched his direct frontal assault, throwing Shaddock forward in a straightaway charge, as Trible and Jepson hammered away at the flanks. Montrill thought how young Cris Herrold would have gloried in the assignment given to

Shaddock. . . . The Indians had dismounted and taken cover to fight back, but the cavalry ripped that dazed red mob apart, rode the warriors under, smashed them back against the bottom of Castle Rock.

The repeating rifles made the difference, Montrill thought. The Apaches had some Henry repeaters but not enough. Mostly they had old single-shot carbines, or bows and lances. This lack of fire-power and leadership was fatal to the Indian cause. Survivors were trying to surrender wholesale now, but some of the fighting-mad troopers went on shooting and slashing them down. Other braves started clawing their way up the cliff, only to be shot off the wall by vengeful cavalrymen. The soldiers had seen too many comrades tortured and slain to show any mercy to this enemy.

It was an overwhelming victory for the army, a crushing defeat for the Apaches. But Hatchese was still at large with the bulk of his force. The campaign was by no means ended, the red menace was yet to be destroyed in Arizona Territory.

K and L had paid a price, however. There were cavalry horses and blue-clothed bodies scattered among the copper-skinned dead. The laughing Vermilya had been right about getting himself killed before he could spend his legacy from Bucky Thackston, and Gilkeson was beyond caring about the three hundred owed to him by the dead Corporal McCord.

Sergeant Kirk, carbine and pistol emptied, was dead in a ring of Apache corpses, and there were others. Turco, who had thought the Indians wouldn't fight; the gloomy Sulima; and Audette, the dapper little Frenchman. . . . Casualties enough, but they were light in comparison to the enemy losses. Virtually the entire Apache force was killed, wounded, or captured. It was enough to cripple Hatchese, perhaps fatally, but not enough to end the war.

Jim Raven, occupied with the field-glasses again, spat explosively and said: "Look down there, boys. There's your blasted Hatchese!" Far to the south and west, across Hellsgate in the direction of Cadnac Cut, a great saffron dust cloud hovered in the heat-shimmering atmosphere. At first, it looked as if Hatchese was coming up to attack from the rear, but after an interval it was apparent that the dust pall was moving away from the desert toward the mountain passes. To the three observers that meant one thing: Hatchese, with probably two hundred bucks, was going to strike back at Fort Burnside itself.

"We'd better hit your cut-off, Jim," said Montrill. "The Old Man will see that and turn back, but never in time to overtake them."

"I reckon," grunted Raven, "we got some ridin' to do."

"There can't be more than a token force left at the post," Ashley said morosely. "A guard detail with the wounded and women."

"Seaver and his boys must be there," Montrill reminded. "That'll help considerably."

Jim Raven grinned. "Not to mention Herrold and Barron. Them two kaydets'll hold the fort for sure!" He laughed barkingly. "Let's mount up and travel, men. Even takin' that short-cut, it's a long ways home."

Brushing off swarms of insects and swinging into the hot leather, they pulled away from the rim and started back across the lofty ochre plateau, their shadows long in the afternoon sunlight. The pleasure in the triumph they had just witnessed was gone, and each man rode somber and indrawn with thoughts of Hatchese and his dog warriors bearing down on an undermanned garrison. Midway of the weirdly sculptured yellow tableland, Jim Raven raised his hand

and they drew rein. "I smell Injuns," Jim said, his eyes pale slitted fire in his dark hawk-face.

They were reaching for their booted carbines when it came with shocking suddenness, the wicked swish of arrows, the whine and snarl of lead, dust spurting, stone splinters flying, cholla clumps bursting, and the reports ringing out raggedly. Montrill heard the sickening sound of that arrow striking Raven, and saw the feathered shaft buried almost to his buckskin chest, the barbed head protruding from his back. Raven's black reared up and caught a bullet and went down thrashing and kicking. Jim fell clear, rifle in hand, and started firing at once from his knees.

Montrill threw his bay gelding down behind the redstone outcroppings, and landed in a balanced crouch with his Winchester blazing. Ashley booted the roan in behind a cluster of boulders, and opened up with his carbine. There were perhaps a dozen Apaches deployed across the inner end of the promontory-like mesa, fading into the rocks and mesquite thickets and ironwood trees, maintaining their fire. Bullets screeched off stony planes and tore up dusty furrows, while arrows clattered, sparking and slithering among the boulders.

Jim Raven crawled to Montrill's side, looking at his dead horse and the arrow that transfixed his chest. "Imagine that?" he said in mild wry disgust. "An arrow. And right in the home stretch, Monty." Montrill had his knife ready to work on the shaft. Raven blew bloody froth from his bearded lips. "Cut her off, Monty, but don't pull her out. Last longer — this way." Montrill nodded and sliced off both ends of the shaft. Ashley was shooting with steady care from his barricade on their left. "Careless," muttered Raven. "Walked right into it. You can't ever stop thinkin' — in this game. Monty, you boys can make that cut-off."

"You'll be with us, Jim." Montrill pressed fresh shells into the rifle.

"Not this time, son. I've got mine. . . . You pull out and drop down the front rim. It ain't too tough or steep."

"We'll hang around awhile, Jim," drawled Montrill.

"You don't show much sense, dammit! After all the time I spent with you, boy." Raven was reloading his carbine, calm and methodical.

"We'll get out of here, Jim."

"Not me, Monty," said Raven. "This is the way — it was writ in the book, for me. I could feel it comin', son."

196

Ashley called from the left flank, loud and clear, without panic: "They're moving in, Rick!"

"H'ist me up, so I can get a crack at 'em," panted Jim Raven. "I still owe the red sons a few licks."

Montrill helped him up against the slanting sandstone, and Raven bit a chew off his plug. "I can take my tobacco now. I'm all right, Monty."

The Apaches were writhing and flitting forward, their ponies left in the rear, firing as they came, using nothing but rifles now. Dirt geysered, stone fragments splintered, and a golden shower seemed to explode in front of Montrill's sun-squinted eyes. Lining his sights and squeezing the trigger, Montrill felt a fierce exultance as the butt slammed his shoulder and a brave in a tailless army shirt pitched headlong into a patch of nopal and wanded ocotillo. Swerving the barrel, Montrill found another target and fired twice, the second shot spilling a bare-torsoed warrior in the white-flowered Spanish bayonet blades. Raven and Ashley were making their slugs count likewise, one Indian screaming and dying in the tarragon, another squirming into stillness at the foot of a pitahaya spire. The rush was broken up and turned back.

Raven grinned at Montrill, but the agony showed in his bleached eagle eyes. "Glad they waited till I saw that show back there, Monty. Worst lickin' Hatchese ever took. . . . You and Ash dust along out, Monty."

"Save your breath, Jim."

"I can hold 'em here. I'll pile 'em up three deep, Monty. It's all I'm good for now. Use your head, boy."

"Maybe we like it here," Montrill said softly. "Here they come again, Jim."

There were more than the dozen he had first estimated, and they came howling this time, with an insane disregard for death. Montrill hitched higher on the redstone, in order to work his carbine faster, and bullets chipped rock in his face and tugged at his torn uniform. Jim Raven reared straight up, firing swiftly until the Winchester was empty. More Apaches were down, but the rest kept coming like madmen. Raven set down the rifle, drew his two Colt .44's, and turned them loose, the guns flaming and bucking in his big hands. This gave Montrill and Ashley time to reload and snatch the extra carbines from their saddles.

Montrill was handing the spare rifle to Raven, when Jim jerked and doubled like a man with stomach cramps, dropping slowly to his knees. Snarling and cursing, Montrill slashed his shots at the fleeting dodging coppery forms, and Ashley poured it on from his rockpile. Smashed to a stop, the Indians scattered and burrowed out of sight once more, in greasewood shrubs and mescal hummocks, their dead strewn along the plateau.

"Now maybe you'll light out!" panted Jim Raven, bloody hands gripping his abdomen. "Get goin', Monty. Somebody's got to get to Burnside!"

Montrill smiled sweatily and shook his bronze head.

"I'm dyin', you damn fool. I don't want nobody around — but dead Injuns."

"They're pulling out, Jim."

"Don't feed me that, boy. They'll be back." Raven was hunched against the rock barrier, clutching his belly, sweat pouring down the ugly face that was twisted and drained-looking. Death already dimmed the gray eyes, marked the gaunt sunken features.

Montrill signaled to Ashley, and Ash ducked across the open space leading his roan past Raven's dead black horse. "Jim," he murmured, kneeling beside the scout. Raven's grin was a pathetic grimace. "Ash, can you get this danged Rebel started outa here?"

"What's the hurry, Jim?" asked Ashley,

trying to keep his voice natural and level.

"I don't need — no audience. Line outa here, for —" Raven's voice broke into a racking strangled cough, and a gush of blood darkened his buckskins. His face set like stone, the eyes fixed and vacant. A brief final spasm shook him, and it was over for Jim Raven. . . . They took his guns, shell belt and wallet, laying him out decently beside the sandstone spur, their eyes and throats filled with bitterness.

"Which way, Rick?" asked Ashley.

"Let them come in again, then break straight through," Montrill decided. "Haven't got time to go way around, Ash."

They waited until the Indians were closer this time, before blasting them with carbine fire, lashing them back into cover. Swinging astride their horses then, revolving pistols in hand, they broke from shelter and drove forward at a full reckless gallop. Surprise and sheer speed carried them past the foremost bucks, guns flashing and lead breathing all about them. A husky painted warrior jumped out of the mesquite, his rifle exploding almost in Montrill's face, but Rick rode him down and Ashley pumped a .44 into him. Brown bodies loomed up and vanished in the muzzle-blasts. The riders hurtled through low on their flattened racing mounts, running away from the braves on foot with bullets whining after them.

At the rear of the plateau, three mounted Apaches burst out of the runted cedars and scrub firs where the ponies were held, their fire leaping at the two officers. Never slackening speed, Montrill and Ashley crashed head on into them with Colts aflame. Montrill blew one off his bare-backed perch, and gunwhipped another to the ground in that stormy plunging welter. Ashley shot the third Indian from his pony, and they thundered on into the trees, routing and chasing off the Apache horses, laughing like maniacs drunk on battle.

As they dropped from the back rim, a mounted Indian sentry crossed in front of them, clay-daubed face stupid with surprise. Montrill rammed his big bay straight into the wiry pony, and chopped his steel barrel across the shaven skull, the impact rippling up his arm. The buck lunged earthward, with Ashley throwing a slug into him for good measure, and they angled down the slope into the forest, the Apache horses stampeding before them. There would be no pursuit from that party.

Once clear of the enemy, Montrill and Ashley struck a southeasterly course into the Osage Mountains toward Jim Raven's short-cut, the headwaters of the Cherokee on the other side, and the plateau of Fort Burnside. It didn't seem right without Jim, and they had a lost lonely feeling, as they slanted away from Hellsgate and the sinking sun. . . . As if a lot of people were missing, all at once.

CHAPTER XV

Fort Burnside drowsed in the spring sunshine, the long parade looking deserted and empty, the whole quadrangle unduly quiet, barren and lifeless. Teresa Thurston was bored to desperation. With Herrold still confined in the guardhouse, there was nobody to spend her time with, no interest to relieve the monotony. She was no longer friendly with Anita Raven, and had nothing in common with Mrs. Jepson and Mrs. Trible. She went to the hospital to volunteer her services, but withdrew when she found Anita already working there.

Tess chatted with Seaver, Crater and Dallas, but they placed her on a pedestal that made her feel uncomfortable and quite unworthy. Some of the younger men from that expedition were real good-looking, she thought. The clean-cut Stonesifer and rugged Lemonick, the blond Ullrich and red-haired Fennell. But they were too conscious of the breach between them and the commanding officer's daughter, all except the Harvard-bred Fennell. . . . And Crispin Herrold had nothing to say to Teresa when she visited the guardhouse.

Finally her thoughts turned to Kirby Tisdale. The foreman had not been back to the post since his clash with Herrold behind officers' row, and that piqued Teresa, as any sign of indifference to her charms always did. She knew Tisdale wasn't afraid of Herrold or any other man. He simply wasn't interested enough to try and resume the courtship. It stung her to think that Tisdale had let her go so easily. Tess recalled, with a sensual stir of excitement, the lesson Kirby had been about to teach her that night. She wondered how far he would have gone, if Herrold hadn't happened along. . . . I'm a little hussy, Teresa Thurston reflected with a certain satisfaction.

It might be an agreeable diversion to ride over to the Forrester ranch. It was only a few miles distant, near the northern end of the plateau. Teresa was confident of being able to bring Kirby Tisdale to heel again, and she wouldn't be contented until she had done so. Once sure of him again, she'd dismiss him with such scathing contempt that Tisdale would smart for weeks and months from it.

Tess was not supposed to leave the stockade unescorted, but the troopers were unable to deny the major's daughter anything, when she flashed that smile and flirted with those roguish dancing blue eyes. In a tailored black riding habit, she went to the stables and had her favorite sorrel saddled. Mounted, she took a back way to pass behind headquarters and avoid the inquisitive gaze of Ray Barron. If he tried to stop her, Tess was ready to slash his bold beaked face open with the quirt old Sergeant Dunleavy had braided for her. . . . The guards were hesitant about letting her outside, but the girl soon prevailed upon them, laughing in exultant freedom when she was beyond the walls, following the cottonwood-lined Cherokee River north toward the Flying F.

The rattling rise and fall of gunfire in the distance brought her to an anxious halt at about the halfway mark, but Teresa Thurston urged the spirited sorrel on as the shooting thinned out and died away. Probably some of Kirby's crazy cowhands letting off steam. But when she breasted a sharp ridge that brought the spread into view, black clouds of smoke laced with scarlet, orange and yellow flames were mushrooming evilly from the ranch building, bunkhouse, barn, and sheds. Shocked and horrified, Tess saw the reddish-brown forms of Indians, mounted and afoot, moving about the burning structures, their yipping cries hideous on the air. Frozen in her saddle, Tess thought: The fort'll be next, with nowhere near enough soldiers to defend it, and that pompous ass of a Barron in command.

Wheeling the sorrel, Tess Thurston started back down the sloping shoulder, but not before she was seen by the Apaches. On the plain, she lifted the gelding into a powerful reaching gallop. Glancing back over her shoulder, Teresa saw four mounted redskins silhouetted briefly on the ridgetop, plunging down the side in pursuit. With luck, the big cavalry horse should stay well ahead of the smaller Indian ponies, but terror was rising to the proportions of panic in the girl. Golden hair streaming under her hat, Tess rode the sorrel at full tilt, the sun-struck landscape skimming past in a yellow-brown blur threaded by the greenery of the riverbanks. When she looked back again, the tough wiry little ponies appeared to be gaining ground, and Tess took to the spurs and quirt.

She estimated the raiding party at forty or fifty, but only four bucks were coming after her. Quite enough, of course. Teresa attempted to gauge the personnel at the post. A dozen or fifteen able-bodied men, apart from Seaver's detail, and several of them in the guardhouse. Another fifteen or twenty sick and wounded in the hospital, perhaps half of them able to fight. The sutler and his helper, a few friendly Indians and their squaws, and four white women. Mrs. Trible and Mrs. Jepson would be useless, but Anita Raven and Teresa herself could handle firearms. . . . It wasn't as hopeless as it first seemed, unless there were more Apaches coming. But the odds were bad enough.

Twisting for another backward glance, Tess was positive the warriors had closed up on her, within range now but holding their fire. They wanted her alive, she supposed, but any minute now they'd be shooting her horse. . . . The sorrel lurched, stumbled, and for a terrible instant Tess thought they were going down, but the great beast recovered and went on, limping a trifle, lathered and blowing hard. He was lamed and slowed from stepping in that hole though, and the Indians were sure to run her down now. Burnside was still a mile or more away.

Teresa glimpsed three more horsemen slanting in from the west, and thought at first they were braves. Then, with a choked cry of relief and gladness, she recognized Kirby Tisdale, Bowie Hulpritt, and another Forrester rider, splashing across the Cherokee shallows and driving on to cut between the girl and her pursuers. She had expected they were all massacred back at the ranch, but these three must have been out on the range and so escaped the raiders.

The Apaches fanned out and started firing, but their marksmanship was poor. Hulpritt threw up his carbine and knocked one pony and rider down in the surging dust. Kirby Tisdale, reins in teeth and six-guns in either hand, raced on in with pistols flaring as the gap shortened. Another buck shrieked and pitched head down to earth, dragged wildly by his runaway pony. The remaining two whirled and fled for the Flying F, under rifle fire from the three cowhands. Teresa Thurston reined up and awaited her benefactors.

"Has your old man gone crazy?" demanded Kirby Tisdale. "Lettin' you out here alone."

"My father's away," she said demurely.

"What's the matter with the rest of them toy soldiers then?"

"Don't blame them, Kirby. It was all my own fault."

"I can believe that," Tisdale said dryly.

Teresa smiled brightly. "I want to thank you three."

'Sure, let's get to the fort. They'll be hittin' that next," Tisdale said grimly, his eyes narrowed to smoky triangles of slate, jaws and cheekbones straining the bronzed skin.

They rode on toward the stockade in silence. Teresa Thurston was trembling all over, her heart fluttering frantically in her bosom, as the reaction set in. She realized that her escape was temporary and Burnside offered but little security in its present state. These three riders made the odds a bit better. They might be able to fight the Apaches off, until her father got back with the main column, but the best Teresa could rouse was a faint glimmer of hope and faith.

At the main gateway, Teresa Thurston spoke crisply to the sentries. "Indians at Forrester's. Bar the gate and pass the word. Close all entrances and report to headquarters!" And she thought, with a slight glow of pride: I'd have made a good officer myself, if I'd been born a boy. . . . They cantered on and reined in before the headquarters building, stepping out of their sweated saddles.

Ray Barron came out on the porch, smoothing his slick hair and frowning at the men with Teresa, still bearing the marks of Herrold's fists. She repeated the warning, and Barron's heavy jaws dropped, his broad face going loose and slack.

"Good Lord, Tess!" gasped Barron. "Indians, *here?* . . . Are you sure?"

"See that smudge in the sky?" Teresa said, pointing north. "They're burning Forrester's now. They'll be here before you know it. Turn the men out of the guardhouse, Ray."

Barron's chin snapped up, his jaws squaring as he shook his sleek head. "No, Tess. I have no authority to do that. They're under arrest and they're staying under arrest."

"This is an emergency!" Teresa said in cold fury. "We'll need every man that can lift a gun!"

Barron drew himself up rigidly. "I'm in command here, Miss Thurston," he stated with finality.

"You're a complete fool!" flared Teresa Thurston.

Barron stared aghast at her. Kirby Tisdale strode forward, smiling scornfully. "This is no time to argue. There's maybe fifty Apaches comin' at us soon. You can't leave anybody locked up, soldier."

Barron glared at him. "I'll have *you* arrested, if you don't shut up and clear out.

No civilian's giving me orders!"

"The army!" Tisdale spat it out like an epithet. "Listen, your greasy hair's goin' to be full of Indians in a few minutes. Turn them soldiers loose!"

"Corporal of the guard!" shouted Barron. "I warned you, cowboy. I'll arrange for the defense of this post. Those prisoners will stay where they are, and you'll be with them!"

"Why, you poor sad son!" Kirby Tisdale struck with sudden lightning speed and savage power at the pouchy jowls. Barron's glossy head went far back in a spray of blood. He landed on his neck and broad shoulders, dust spouting between the planks as his legs settled widely asprawl on the duckboards. Tisdale stood over him, hands ready, but Barron remained flat on his back, motionless and unconscious.

"Army officers," muttered Tisdale. "Get the keys, Tess, and we'll open up the jailhouse. Got to move fast, gal."

At Teresa Thurston's direction, a grinning corporal of the guard unlocked the cells in the guardhouse. "I can die happy now," he said. "Worth a ninety-day furlough to see Barron get it!" The prisoners poured out and quickly learned the situation. Corporal Magill and Hightower and others, including

Lieutenant Crispin Herrold.

"The luck of the Scots!" Magill said. "And ol' Kirk thought he was the only lucky one. Come on, lads; let's get our rifles." He led the enlisted men on the run toward their quarters.

"Thank you, Tess," said Herrold, as they walked back to headquarters. Then, seeing Barron sprawled senseless on the veranda, he smiled for the first time in days and turned to Tisdale. "And thank you, Kirby. Barron must be getting used to this."

"A pleasure," Tisdale grinned, shaking hands with him. "What was you in for anyway?"

Herrold's smile broadened. "For doing what you just did to Lieutenant Barron."

Tisdale laughed aloud. "That's all right, soldier. Maybe you and me'll get along good now."

"I hope so," Herrold said.

"Kirby did it with one punch, Cris," chided Teresa.

"Perhaps I softened Barron up some, Tess," said Herrold, laughing. "Give a man a little credit."

Teresa Thurston regarded him wonderingly, never having seen Herrold so young and alive, gay and friendly. "You're in command, Cris."

"Thanks to you two. I'll try and justify your judgment."

In the adjutant's office, Herrold strapped on his pistol belt, thrust an extra Colt under it, and took a carbine from the rack, while Teresa and Tisdale detailed the conditions and circumstances for him.

Outside, with troopers straggling in from their posts of duty or the barracks, Herrold assigned two of them to help Barron to the hospital and went on studying the sun-bright rectangle. "Can't keep them outside the walls," he mused. "Have to make our stand in one building. The hospital, I'd say." He scanned the solid compact adobe structure on its slight elevation at the far south-western corner of the stockade. "There the wounded can help, and we can protect them. . . ." Herrold raised his voice: "We're fighting from the hospital. Carry all the guns, ammunition, food, supplies, water, and equipment that you can transport there. On the double! Sergeant Papit in command. . . .

"Sergeant Seaver, take charge of the receiving depot at the hospital. Corporal Magill, select a detail to transfer the horses and gear from the stables and corrals to the hospital basement. Corporal Ettinger, take three men and remove the filing cabinets from headquarters to the hospital office. Everybody make it fast now!"

Herrold turned to Teresa. "Tess, see that the ladies get to the hospital, with their most valuable possessions. Have Anita bring all of Jim's guns. Perhaps Hulpritt and his friend here will assist you." Teresa and the two cowhands moved toward officers' row at once. Kirby Tisdale was watching Herrold with surprise, admiration and respect.

"I reckon it's a good thing the army's got some like you, Cris," said Tisdale.

Herrold smiled strangely. "Thanks, Kirby. That's the highest tribute I've received in the service. About the only one, in fact." He laughed quietly. "Let's call on the sutler. A little whiskey may come in handy during the siege."

Buss was in a frenzy, trying to figure out what to save and what to sacrifice. "Ruined," he groaned. "Ruined by them red hellhounds! Work of a lifetime gone down the drain. All these goods of mine!"

"Worry about savin' your hair, friend," suggested Tisdale.

"Two cases of your best whiskey for the hospital," Herrold said. "And leave out a few kegs of that rotgut you sell for the Indians. It might save us the trouble of killing some of them."

"Who's payin' for this, Lieutenant?"

"The army," Herrold said, calling in two privates to transport the liquor. "If there's any army left in Arizona."

Buss moaned in abject misery. "You might's well take all of it you can lug. The army'll maybe pay sometime. Certainly the Apaches never will!"

"Anythin' to oblige," drawled Kirby Tisdale. Grinning, they hoisted a case apiece and moved on toward the hospital.

Cris Herrold, sweating under his burden, felt better than he had in a long time, happy and elated in the face of the impending crisis. The post was in his command, its defense up to him. The chance he had thought was lost forever had come at last. An opportunity to save the garrison, to redeem himself and his family name. A selfish way to look at their predicament, but Herrold could not help that. He was keyed to razor keenness, every sense and instinct sharpened and alert.

Teresa Thurston was coming across the parade with Mrs. Jepson, Mrs. Trible, and the rider named Andruss, all of them loaded down like pack-mules with personal belongings. Anita Raven and Bowie Hulpritt emerged from the log cabin carrying clothing and firearms. Troopers were rushing back and forth between the hospital and the armory, mess hall, barracks, bakeshop, and the quartermaster's. In the hospital Seaver was supervising the placement of goods, equipment and personnel. The basement was already jammed with nervous horses and forage. Herrold and Tisdale deposited their cargo in the doctor's office, along with the headquarters files, stacked carbines, boxes of ammunition and provisions.

Dr. Halversen, a lively harried bantam of a man with curly gray hair and a waxed black mustache, smiled absently at them. "Hello, Crispin. You're in command, I take it. Barron has a broken jaw. . . . They thought I was insane when I requested a building like this. Had a devil of a time getting it, but the investment's going to pay off today. As if it hadn't already. Glad you thought of the whiskey; it will serve as an anesthetic." He bounced off, a wispy figure full of springy vigor and nervous energy.

Herrold set about checking the disposition of men and arms, placing sharpshooters in the key spots, stationing troopers at every window so that all angles of approach would be covered. The men sensed a difference in young Hellfire this afternoon and obeyed his orders with new alacrity. The boy had changed; the guard-

216

house must have done him good, they told one another. He was more like Montrill now.

The seriously wounded were bedded down in the inner rooms, and the walking wounded had taken firing positions in the sick bay. Lafferty, his leg in a cast, was sitting up in a bed pushed close to a window, fondling a carbine and smiling pleasantly. "The Apaches sure like us," he remarked to Parilli, on crutches nearby. "They follow us right home, kid." Parilli's white teeth flashed. "They'll wish they hadn't!" Rocky Flint leaned on another sill, his arm in a sling, talking casually to Lemonick, whose shoulder was bandaged.

Everyone was inside the adobe walls now, the great oaken front doors locked and barred, the riflemen in place around the interior, with extra carbines, revolvers and shells in easy reach. Mrs. Trible and Mrs. Jepson had refuge in Halversen's small inside laboratory, while Anita Raven and Tess Thurston were standing by to reload firearms and help with the wounded. The friendly Indians of the fort had been segregated in the cellar with the horses, except for a pair of old bucks who wanted to fight against Hatchese.

Herrold made his quiet rounds with

Seaver, offering suggestions here and there, acting on Seaver's advice in certain instances. The soldiers marveled at the transformation in the rash headstrong young officer. Never had they seen Cris Herrold so easy and relaxed, calm and sure, balanced and steady. The master of himself and the whole situation. It was as if he had matured overnight, and the men acquired poise and confidence from the mere sight of him.

Teresa Thurston watched Herrold with love and pride in her blue eyes. With the tension gone from his eyes, mouth and manner, Herrold was handsomer than ever, almost beautiful, his features finely carved and serene, his dark head high but no longer arrogant. Like a slim shining rapier, she thought, delicate and graceful but strong and deadly.

Anita Raven observed the change in Herrold with something like awe, wishing that Jim and Rick Montrill and the others could see him now. She had outgrown her infatuation for Herrold, outlived her pain at his desertion, but Anita found that she liked and respected him — for the first time. It occurred to her that Cris Herrold had waited all his life for a moment such as this, perhaps this very one. When it came he was all at once man-grown, tempered and restrained, ready to meet it.

Dr. Halversen's office projected turret-like into the rectangle, and in the strategic bay windows there Tex Dallas, Charley Crater and Red Fennell had taken their stand to cover the entire front area. They would also bear the brunt of enemy fire. Old Seaver smiled at them, leathery cheeks creasing to faded squinting blue eyes.

"You boys keep out of that whiskey now," he grumbled.

"Why you think we picked this place, Seav?" drawled Dallas, whiplike figure bristling with Colt hand-guns and draped with shell belts.

Herrold stepped forward to look over Fennell's bandaged red head and out across the scorched parade ground. The first Apaches were just thrusting their black scalplocks and paint-striped faces over the top of the stockade behind the 'dobe boxes of officers' row.

"There they are, gentlemen," Herrold murmured mildly. "Business will pick up in a short while, I believe."

Old Seaver was scrutinizing Herrold narrowly, smiling and nodding his approval. He called us gentlemen — and truly meant it. The kid's come of age, and a good thing for all of us that he was left behind in the brig. Imagine Barron in command here. . . . We'd still be floundering around like fish out of water, all over the post.

Herrold lifted his voice, loud and clear. "Hold your fire and your positions, men. We'll let them come to us."

He hoped Hatchese was with them, and all the worst of the bad ones. Herrold always felt that he had a private issue to settle with Hatchese, who had been with Geronimo at the Aravaipa, whose uncle Cochise had massacred Colonel Justin Herrold's command on the Querhada.

CHAPTER XVI

The Indians, sated with the slaughter at Forrester's ranch, were in no hurry. The vanguard scaled the wall and opened the main gate at the northeast corner, diagonally opposite the hospital. The rest pranced in on their ponies, and Seaver had the binoculars trained on them. "No Hatchese, none of the big chiefs," he said. "Bunch of young bucks out on a spree."

The warriors took a childish delight in gaining entrance to this elaborate stronghold of the Great White Father, whom they despised as a double-tongued breaker of treaties. Perceiving that the fort was unoccupied save for the hospital at the far end, they proceeded to search and explore with child-like curiosity, prowling, prying, tearing things apart, like the natural-born vandals they were. Smashing window glass and destroying property with infantile glee, dancing and capering about. Now and then they paused to fire long-range shots and hurl unintelligible insults at the adobe walls and high deep-silled windows of the hospital.

After spreading havoc and destruction in post headquarters and the barracks, the Apaches set fire to those wooden buildings with torches, howling in diabolical joy as the flames roared up and smoke billowed. The mess hall, bakery, the sutler's store, stables and sheds went next, while the onlooking troopers ground their teeth and bit off curses, and Buss ranted hysterically until Corporal Magill silenced him. The sun-dried boards blazed up fast and furious, the smoke clouds blackening the brassy brightness of the sky, and the air was tainted with the dark vile stench of burning timber.

By this time the Indians were drunk on the cheap raw whiskey left by the sutler. Unable to burn the 'dobes of officers' row, they ransacked them from end to end, ripping and rending everything that was breakable, firing the wrecked interiors, bedecking themselves in feminine finery and cavorting like idiots. Teresa Thurston said: "I don't think my dresses are very becoming to them," and she was smiling bravely. Anita Raven felt grateful when the raiders turned back before reaching her cabin. Not that she had much to lose, but it was home to Jim and her.

Then, crazed with more alcohol, the lust for blood heightened to a fever pitch, the Apaches moved toward the hospital, the vast bonfires roaring briskly behind them, dense smoke screening their advance. Grim-jawed slit-eyed cavalrymen were alerted at the windows, from which the glass had been broken. Rocky Flint, splinted left arm resting on the broad sill, cocked a revolver and breathed his old prize-fighter's invitation: "Come on, come on and fight. Come in and get it!"

They came creeping and skulking, then hurtled forward with drunken yells and suicidal abandon, slamming shots at the high windows. Lips thinned on teeth, the soldiers opened fire, sheeted flames springing from the adobe walls as they triggered and levered the Winchester .44 repeater carbines. Shattering that mad assault, dropping bucks on all sides of the structure, driving the others back, leaving ragged windrows of coppery bodies littered along the sunbaked, fire-stained earth.

Falling back the Indians resorted to the more sensible tactics of sniping from cover. It was more effective than charging, even though they had foolishly burned their closest and most substantial shelters, and the deep-ledged windows of the hospital afforded good protection. But with rifles and bows constantly hammering at those apertures, the warriors were bound to score some hits and reduce the small garrison. It went on through the long sweltering afternoon and into the night, for the Apaches were too fired-up with liquor and bloodlust to cease hostilities because of darkness.

Lieutenant Herrold and Sergeant Seaver and Kirby Tisdale seemed to be everywhere in that powder-reeking interior, from the large main ward on the north to the office turret at the southern end. . . . When four drink-inflamed maniacs came at the main door with a battering-ram, those three were on the spot to strip the brown bodies off that pole with a withering blast, as autumn leaves are shorn from a branch by a gust of wind.

The wounded were giving an excellent account of themselves, but Lafferty had died firing from his bed, a faint trace of that smile still on his pleasant face, rumpled head bent as if he had dozed off over the carbine. And Rocky Flint, fighting with his left arm in a sling, had to retire when his right shoulder was smashed by a slug. Young Parilli fell with an arrow piercing his throat, the second of the survivors of that death march with Seaver to die back here in the home cantonment.

Anita Raven and Tess Thurston aided Halversen in caring for the wounded, both old and new. And the little doctor strove to ignore the damage being done to his beloved hospital.

In the office that night, Red Fennell, scion of an old Cambridge family, had just rendered a classic toast and drained a cup of whiskey — "Purely medicinal, boys" — when a stray bullet struck him exactly between the eyes. Kirby Tisdale took his place at the bay windows with Crater and Dallas.

Ray Barron, his broken jaw bound tightly, had not risen from his cot to take part in any of the defense. The raging hatred that smouldered in him was directed against Herrold and Tisdale, rather than the Indians.

Despite the casualties, Herrold was convinced that they could hold out indefinitely against these attackers. The Apaches must have at least a third of their number killed or wounded already, and the rest were too drunk to be fully effective. Unless more Indians arrived, ahead of Major Thurston, the defenders were relatively secure in their fortress-like adobe.

■ ■ ■ ■

Late that night, the fighting subsided, the quadrangle in stillness, and the garrison resting in relays, Herrold was drinking black coffee laced with whiskey in the kitchen, when Hightower reported that someone was calling from the stockade at the rear of the hospital. "Sounds like a white man all right, sir. But we don't want to take any chances."

Herrold followed him to a back window and listened intently. A low hoarse voice came from the black-shadowed wall across a moonlit expanse to the hospital terrace. "Hallo-oo, the fort. I need help out here. Can you send it?"

"Who's there?" Herrold called back.

"Montrill — and Ashley."

Something jumped in Herrold's chest and constricted his throat. Hightower swore with hushed gladness, "Monty and Ash!" Herrold threw his voice out again, with an effort: "Climb over and come in."

"Can't make it. Ash is wounded," Montrill's southern drawl came.

There was a gate behond the hospital, but the Indians hadn't opened this one yet. It would have to be unbarred from the inside. . . . "Be ready to move," Herrold

226

advised. "We'll open up for you." It was about fifty yards to the stockade, a long way if any Apaches were watching.

"Volunteers," Herrold said, choking down the bitterness that Montrill's return raised in his throat. "Two with side-arms to unbar the gate and carry the wounded man. Two with carbines to cover them."

Hightower and big Ox Hendree spoke at once, with little Tut Jarnigan and Stonesifer chiming in immediately afterward. Herrold instructed the first two to leave their rifles behind and check their handguns. The second pair had their Winchesters ready. Herrold picked up a spare carbine. "I'll go along with the detail."

"Sir, let me go instead," said Ullrich. "They need you here, sir."

Herrold smiled, with a knot aching in back of his tongue. "Thank you, Ullrich. But I'll be all right."

They stepped out the rear door and down the gentle grade. The moonlight seemed unnaturally brilliant, and they felt exposed and naked. Two dead braves were stretched on the crusted soil, but no live ones opened fire on them. The stockade shadow was welcome indeed. Hightower and Hendree drew the bars and flung open the gate. Montrill was standing over Ashley, revolver in hand, and two halfdead horses slumped nearby.

The first two troopers lifted Ashley between them, and Montrill led the mounts inside. Stonesifer and Jarnigan relocked the portal and turned to cover the others. The return trip was even slower and longer, the moonlight surely making them visible for miles. Herrold and Montrill exchanged terse explanations on the way, expecting bullets at every stride. But none came, nothing happened.

With Ashley borne away to the doctor and the horses stabled in the basement, Herrold and Montrill were left alone inside the dim rear vestibule, the old antagonism rising between them. Herrold felt all he had built up and become crumbling away in Montrill's presence, leaving nothing but a bitter flame of resentment and hatred. This man had shot his brother down, and now he'd come back to snatch away Herrold's final opportunity. Herrold had always known that some day they'd face one another across gun barrels. Now, in his blind unreasoning rage, Herrold thought the time had come.

"You've done a good job here, Cris," said Montrill, scouring his bronze-bearded jaws with a big grimy hand.

"Never mind that," Herrold said tautly.

"There's something else, Montrill."

"What's eating you, boy?"

Herrold leaned his carbine on the wall and backed off, black eyes fixed on the other man. "You've got a gun there. Use it, mister!"

"You're crazy," Montrill said. "I don't want this command. You rank me anyway — remember? All I want is somethin' to drink and eat, and a place to sleep."

Herrold laughed. "I've got nothing to lose. I'm up for courtmartial. You murdered my brother, mister, and you've lived too long!"

Montrill sighed wearily. "I didn't kill your brother. But he had something to do with getting mine killed. Leave me alone now. I'm too tired for this nonsense!" His eyes were pure green now.

"Who did kill Dirk then?"

"The man is dead," Montrill said slowly. "Haven't you got enough Indians to fight here?"

"You're lying!" Herrold accused. "Reach for that gun. Let's have an end to this."

Montrill smiled sadly. "With that holster flap, you wouldn't have a chance. The man who shot your brother is dead — as dead as both our brothers. Knock it off now, or I'll pistol-whip hell out of you!" Montrill strode forward, shouldered the slighter man aside, and went on, lurching in exhaustion, on the verge of dropping in his tracks.

Herrold came to his senses then, shame and pity welling up in him. "Wait a minute, Rick." He hastened after the rangy Southerner. "I'm sorry, Rick. I guess I was crazy."

"Forget it, boy. And find me a drink somewhere." Montrill's grin was ghastly, and he weaved on sagging knees, uniform in ribbons.

"Will you share the command?" asked Herrold, suddenly like a small boy trying to make amends for misbehaving.

"Not me, Cris," said Montrill. "I'm practically a stretcher case. Just get me some whiskey and water." His eyes had turned gray and tired.

"Anything you want, mister," Herrold said, smiling with quiet humility, hurrying on ahead to the office.

Anita Raven came running along the murky corridor into Montrill's arms, and then almost had to support him as he reeled under her weight. "Rick! Where's Jim?" she cried, and then stricken understanding spread on her dark lovely features. "I know. Jim's dead — isn't he?" Montrill nodded gravely and held the girl, as she crumpled sobbing in his arms.

Teresa Thurston approached, more slowly

and sedately. "Any news of my father, Rick?"

"He's all right, Tess," Montrill said across the black sheen of Nita's hair. "They smashed the Apaches below Castle Rock. Ought to be back here in a day or two."

"Thank heaven!" said Teresa. "And thank you, Rick. Can I help Anita? . . ."

"Maybe," Montrill murmured. "I'm not much of a comfort."

"Poor dear Rick," said Anita brokenly, turning from him to be enfolded in Teresa's embrace, the two women walking away together.

Ox Hendree came lumbering back from the operating room. "Ash's goin' to be all right, Monty. Put the Vermonters in front, they used to say."

"That one belongs in front, Ox," said Montrill.

"Him and you both, Monty." Hendree grinned and moved on to his post.

Herrold returned with a whiskey bottle and a glass of water, and Montrill promptly sampled them in turn. "Ah, that's fine." He started to sink down against the wall.

"Come on, Rick. Halversen wants to look you over and put you to bed."

"Only place for me," Montrill mumbled, swaying forward on Herrold's shoulder.

"Thought I'd been tired before. Never like this."

It seemed as if half the people he knew in the world were dead, and the rest of them likely to die within the next twenty-four hours. But there was no need of telling these folks that Hatchese was on his way with a big war party. Nothing they could do about it. Nothing anybody could do but wait. Fight it out to the finish, hope and pray, if you hadn't forgotten how.

Chapter XVII

At dawn it began all over again. . . . The Apaches were soberer, smarter and stronger by daybreak, inflicting severe punishment on the defenders, but the army rifles went on taking an even heavier toll of enemy lives.

Montrill hauled himself out of bed at nine, gulping coffee spiked with whiskey, bathing, shaving, dressing in fresh clean clothes from the quartermaster's supply. He looked fairly human once more, but was far from feeling well and strong. After visiting Ashley and other wounded men, Montrill relieved Herrold, who had been up all night. Wandering around the hospital then, Montrill swapped greetings and stories with all the troopers, and it was like old home week for an interval, or a reunion of men returned from the dead.

The raiders were at the sutler's rotgut again, and their attack diminished accordingly. They had lost fifty per cent of their force, Seaver estimated, and were getting a bellyful of fighting as well as whiskey. The army riflefire was too accurate and rapid to withstand. By noon the Indians were thoroughly sick of attacking, and even sicker from swilling whiskey. As the heat of that second afternoon increased to an intolerable degree, the decimated warriors were about ready to give up and slink off in defeat.

Then Montrill saw something that chilled him with horror and despair, although it was the inevitable sight he had been expecting. A great long column of horsemen streamed in through the main entrance, most of them naked to the loins and daubed with colored clay, shrilling war cries and brandishing rifles, bows and lances, as they swarmed the northern end of the rectangle. Hatchese himself was leading them with the air of a world conqueror, and perhaps a hundred and fifty picked braves were at his heels.

This was no drunken rabble bent on loot and plunder, but a military unit on a well-plotted crusade, commanded by a born strategist and inspirational leader. Hatchese dispatched one band outside to attack from the south and west stockade walls. He deployed another down officers' row and as far as the Raven cabin. A third and more fluid force advanced along the blackened ruins of the barracks. Hatchese and his cavalry sat back behind the charred debris of headquarters, waiting to sweep forward in the final assault. . . . It's just a matter of time now, Montrill thought. They've got until the Old Man returns with K and L, and we'll never last that long.

Herrold came up beside Montrill and Seaver, staring around the quadrangle with swollen reddened eyes. "Well, we've got them all now," he said wryly, smiling and elbowing Montrill. "Did I give you the impression that I wanted this command, Rick?"

Shortly after three o'clock the attack opened, and this time it was conducted with systematic skill and disciplined efficiency. Apparently each group of Indian snipers had certain designated windows to concentrate on, for bullets and arrows came pouring through in steady torrents, the lead shrieking and the shafts whirring.

The depth of the windows was no longer adequate. Corporal Magill was shot through the head, and Private Panghorst died with a flaming arrow in his chest. Andruss, the Flying F rider, went down with three bullet-holes in his body. . . . Soon many of the sills were untenable, and Herrold warned men down and away from them. The interior of the hospital, hazed with smoke and stone dust, became an inferno of fiery arrows and screeching slugs. Hightower and Jarnigan were wounded by ricochets. The place reeked of powder and blood and death.

"Down, everybody down!" Herrold ordered. "Wait until they rush."

But the Indians weren't ready to charge yet. They went on drilling away at the apertures in the adobe walls, keeping the army pinned down under constant and growing pressure. Montrill, stamping out patches of fire from the blazing arrows, sent Anita Raven and Tess Thurston back to inner safety, and thought what a brutal ending this was for two young ladies like that.

The afternoon wore blisteringly on, shadows stretching across the parade as the sun descended in the west. Sunset painted the horizon above the far-flung Osages, and still the Apaches did not come to the attack. Twilight laid a soft silver haze in the air, with lavender and blue shadows spreading on the land. Dusk gathered and thickened, and then the abrupt desert night closed in, with stars aglitter and a shrinking curved moon like a bloodied saber in the sky.

They'll come in the darkness, thought

Montrill. They'll fight any time, do anything, for that Hatchese.

The Indians had ceased firing, and were no doubt preparing for the final onslaught. Time was running swiftly out for the shocked, numbed men and women in the battered adobe hospital.

"If they get in here, Cris," said Montrill, "we ought to take care of the ladies."

"Yes, we'll have to," Herrold agreed dully. "Let's get a drink while we can, Rick."

They were in Halversen's office drinking whiskey and waiting for the last big assault, when a familiar stirring sound floated on the night breeze, more vibrant and thrilling than ever before. The brass call of trumpets, high and clear in the desert night, the most welcome music Montrill had ever heard.

"Glory be to God!" rasped old Seaver, in hoarse awed tones.

And then they were laughing and yelling at the windows, watching the cavalry drive into the quadrangle and shatter the Apaches into wild scattered flight. Even Hatchese's hand-picked warriors weren't standing against two troops of United States Regulars, K and L of the Third Regiment. Snarling swearing troopers, lean-jawed, flaming-eyed, and crazy mad at seeing their post in charred rubble, blasted braves from the ponies and thundered over them after more victims. Rode them down on all sides, killed them left and right, shot and sabered and trampled Indian bodies under steelshod hoofs. It was an utter and murderous rout, without quarter or mercy.

Still watching the savage welter at the north end, Montrill became aware of some presence behind him, and instinctively reached for his open-sheathed Colt as he wheeled smoothly from the window. Ray Barron stood spread-legged in the doorway, jaws and head bound like a mummy, madness shining in his wicked eyes and broad face, the pistol in his heavy hand leveled at Herrold's back.

"Drop it, you fool!" yelled Montrill, lining his own revolver.

Everyone came about reaching for weapons, but Barron saw nobody but Cris Herrold in the vague smoky light. Orange fire burst roaring across the cluttered room, and Herrold rocked back on the windowsill, his gun half-drawn, surprise and disgust on his handsome features. Montrill pressed his trigger then, the .44 flaming and lifting in his hand, and Kirby Tisdale threw down with both guns blazing at Barron's hulk. The impacts jolted Barron backward, his pistol exploding at the ceiling, and he fell twisting across the threshold, kicked and groaned once, and stirred no more.

Montrill glanced at the windows, but Herrold had fallen backwards and dropped outside. "The kid's gone," Tex Dallas said. "And just when he got to be a man."

Charley Crater spat tobacco juice at Barron's boots, and old Seaver shook his gray head sorrowfully. Kirby Tisdale cursed viciously and eyed his smoking guns. "Must be slowin' up with these irons, to let a tinhorn like that get a slug into Cris." They turned back to observing the ebbtide of battle in the north.

Montrill walked to the window and leaned over the wide sill. He saw nothing in the shadows directly below, but caught a lurching movement out at the bottom of the terrace. Swinging lithely over the sill, Montrill dropped to the ground, staggering and starting down the slope. Herrold was alive and moving, stumbling onto the parade in a daze.

At that moment a lone rider came hurtling down the parade ground, an Indian on an unshod horse, bent on escaping through the south gate. There were no cavalrymen after this one. In a glimmer of moonlight, Montrill glimpsed the Apache in an old officer's coat, the predatory beak and down-clamped mouth of Hatchese. Lifting his Colt, Montrill started firing, but the chief and his pony seemed impervious to bullets. Herrold was shooting too, but horse and rider came galloping on untouched, unhittable. Montrill wished he had brought a carbine.

What the devil is this? thought Montrill, running forward. Hatchese can't make medicine that strong. . . . If he gets away this war will go on forever. . . . Montrill lined shots at the fleeing horseman, until the hammer clicked on a spent shell. There was no time to reload either. But the pony was faltering in stride, floundering, rolling in a silvery dust storm, and Hatchese was flung clear, bounding upright as Herrold reeled toward him.

Hatchese's powerful right arm lashed out in a throwing motion, and steel spun a thin vivid line in the moonlight. Herrold jerked backward and nearly went over, as the knife blade drove deep into his breast. Swaying on spraddled legs and trying to lift his gunhand, Herrold fell gasping to his knees.

Hatchet in hand, the big Apache chief was coming at him, as Herrold straightened and strove to bring the barrel of his Colt level. Hatchese was almost on top of him, ready for the stroke that would cleave his skull to the throat, when Herrold finally got his gun up and squeezed the trigger. Flame ripped the Indian's great body, stabbed him into a slow backward stagger. He snarled and threw the ax, but without aim or strength.

On his feet now, Herrold held the revolver with both hands, and it roared again with bright lancing fire. Hatchese's face seemed to vanish in that muzzle-blast. He landed on his back, heaved convulsively, shuddered into stillness and death, his shattered features in the dirt of Burnside.

"There, by God!" panted Crispin Herrold: *"There! . . ."* Dropping the gun that was too heavy for both hands now, he groped weakly for the haft of the knife in his chest, tugged at it. The effort was too much. With a long weary sigh Herrold slumped earthward, but Montrill caught him and eased him down gently. Herrold looked up and smiled faintly. "Rick? I got him. . . . The big one, Hatchese."

"Sure, you got him, Cris. You got him all right."

"No courtmartial — for this Herrold." He smiled and died, in Montrill's arms.

That's the way they found them, when it was all over: Hatchese dead with his face against the ground, Cris Herrold dead with his curly head on Montrill's lap. Montrill got up slowly and trailed some of the troopers back toward the hospital. Anita Raven came out to meet him and they clung together for a moment in the shadows, mouth to mouth, her firm flowing body crushed against his rangy frame.

Major Thurston stood before the front door with his arm around Teresa, talking to Dr. Halversen, Sergeant Seaver, Kirby Tisdale, and others. "So that's really Hatchese down there? Well, this ought to keep the Indians down in Arizona, for a time at least. . . . Who's the trooper there with Hatchese?"

"The man who saved what's left of this fort," Kirby Tisdale said.

"Lieutenant Herrold, sir," said Seaver. "We was lucky to have him, Major. Never could of held on without that boy. And he got Hatchese — all by himself."

"A fine officer," agreed Dr. Halversen. "A very gallant gentleman."

"I'm certainly glad to hear that," Thurston said. "I knew he was a good soldier. I'm happy to learn that he proved himself as an Indian fighter, too."

Teresa was sobbing quietly on her father's shoulder. "If that doesn't clear the name of Herrold, Dad, nothing under heaven ever will."

Major Thurston patted her bent blonde head. "It will do it, Tess. I'll see that his name is honored in every army post in the country."

Montrill came up and saluted. Thurston shook hands with him and said: "Fine work all around, Rick."

"Herrold did the job here, Major."

"That's what everyone tells me. But I know what a job you did in the field." Thurston smiled warmly. "And I imagine you were useful here, Rick."

"Thank you, Major," said Montrill. "I'll report in full later."

Thurston nodded. "No hurry — now. The first thing will be burial details. And then we've got a lot of rebuilding to do here."

Montrill and Anita Raven walked away from the hospital, crossing toward her cottage, skirting the bodies of Herrold and Hatchese. There should be peace and security here for a while, but the price for it had been a terrible one. It seemed as if half their world was gone.

"Jim asked me to take care of you, Nita," said Montrill.

"Do you want to? Or do you feel it's your duty, Rick?"

Montrill laughed softly. "Duty, of course. But I'm a duty-loving man."

She smiled and lifted the full ripeness of her lips to his. . . .

At the hospital, which was headquarters now, officers were naming off burial details. Old Sergeant Seaver shifted his tobacco from one leathery cheek to the other, and gestured to where Herrold lay.

"I'll take care of that boy myself. Served with his father and brother. Friend of the family, you might say," Seaver said gruffly.

Charley Crater and Tex Dallas volunteered to assist him. Tess Thurston and Kirby Tisdale followed silently after them, in the vast sparkling Arizona night.

ABOUT THE AUTHOR

Roe Richmond was born Roaldus Frederick Richmond in Barton, Vermont. Following graduation from the University of Michigan in 1933, Richmond found jobs scarce and turned to writing sports stories for the magazine market. In the 1930s he played semi-professional baseball and worked as a sports editor on a newspaper. After the Second World War, Richmond turned to Western fiction and his name was frequently showcased on such magazines as *Star Western, Dime Western,* and *Max Brand's Western Magazine.* His first Western novel, *Conestoga Cowboy,* was published in 1949. As a Western writer, Richmond's career falls into two periods. In the 1950s, Richmond published ten Western novels and among these are his most notable work, *Mojave Guns* (1952), *Death Rides the Dondrino* (1954), *Wyoming Way* (1958), and in 1961 *The Wild Breed.* Nearly an eighteen-year hiatus followed during which Richmond worked as copy editor and proofreader for a typesetting company. Following his retirement, he resumed writing. Greg Tobin, an editor at Belmont Tower, encouraged Richmond to create the Lash Lashtrow Western series. In these original paperback novels, Richmond was accustomed to go back and rework short novels about Jim Hatfield that he had written for *Texas Rangers* magazine in the 1950s. When Tobin became an editor at Bantam Books, he reprinted most of Richmond's early novels in paperback and a collection of his magazine fiction, *Hang Your Guns High!* (1987). Richmond's Western fiction is notable for his awareness of human sexuality in the lives of his characters and there is a gritty realism to his portraits of frontier life.